# A Very Married Christmas

A Silver Bell Falls Holiday Novella

# SAMANTHA CHASE

Copyright © 2017 Samantha Chase

All rights reserved.

ISBN: 978-1979237345

Copyright 2017 Samantha Chase

All Rights Reserved.

No part of this book, with the exception of brief quotations for book reviews or critical articles, may be reproduced or transmitted in any form or by an means, electronic or mechanical, including photocopying, recording, or by any information storage and retrieval system without express written permission from the author.

This is a work of fiction. Names, characters, places, and incidents are the product of the author's imagination or are used fictitiously, and any resemblance to actual persons, living or dead, business establishments, events, or locales is entirely coincidental.

ISBN: 978-1979237345

Publisher: Chasing Romance, Inc.
Editors: Jillian Rivera and Elizabeth Wright
Cover: Designs by Dana
Print formatting: Kim Brooks

## To My Favorite Romance Chasers

What an amazing year this has been! You ladies are such a blessing and an encouragement to me and I am so thankful each and every day for you!!

Thank you for sharing posts, writing reviews and being there when I have crazy questions or need feedback on covers or plots. These books are for you.

Now let's head back to Silver Bell Falls...

# A Very Married Christmas

# Chapter One

"Okay, that's the last of it."

Looking around the room, Melanie Harper sighed with relief before turning and smiling at her fiancé. "I didn't think it would ever get done!"

With a smile of his own, Josiah Stone walked over and wrapped his arms around her waist. "These things take some time, Mel," he said, placing a kiss on the tip of her nose. Hugging her close, he rested his head on top of hers. "Although I have to admit, this did take a bit longer than I thought too."

"I still can't believe the house is done and everything's here and unpacked and…"

"I know," he said softly. "We're home."

It had taken almost two years, but here they were. When Melanie first came to Silver Bell Falls—completely under protest—she never thought this would be where she was going to live for the rest of her life. And yet…here she was. Who knew that by her grandmother leaving her a cabin and the enormous property it sat on that Melanie would find not only a home, but the love of her life.

And Josiah was certainly that.

Stepping out of his arms, she went and sat on their new sofa and patted the spot next to her for him to join her. "Do you remember the day we met?"

With a husky laugh, Josiah sat beside her. "It's burned into my brain. You, naked in the tub of the cabin…" He let out an appreciative sigh.

She swatted his arm playfully. "Not that part," she softly chided. "I mean…did you think this was where we'd end up?"

"At the time, all I was thinking was how I was going to have to haul you down to the station and arrest you for trespassing." He grinned. "In a towel."

They'd talked about their infamous meeting so many times and no matter how serious she tried to be about it, Josiah always had a way of turning it around and sounding like an adorable perv.

"Let's try this again," she said with a dramatic sigh. "I can't believe I came here and was so convinced it was going to be the worst thing to ever happen to me and it turned out to be the exact opposite. I mean, look how far we've come!"

One look at his face and Melanie knew he was still thinking of the bathtub scene so she quickly continued talking.

"We've built a house, Josiah. Our dream

house! We renovated the old cabin and even made good use of your tiny house!"

"Your dad adjusted to tiny living better than I thought he would."

That was true. John Harper had followed his daughter to Silver Bell Falls—a place he had frequented growing up—and jumped at the opportunity to take over Josiah's tiny house. It meant he was close by and it gave him a place of his own until he decided where he wanted to live permanently. It was only a few months ago that he decided to build a house.

"I kind of miss seeing it out there," she said. "There was something comforting about coming home and it being right outside our door."

"I don't think it was the house as much as it was having your dad right there. But he's not so far away now, Mel. He's just on the far side of the property."

She shrugged. "It feels a lot farther. And there's a lot of woods between our house and his."

Josiah moved closer and wrapped an arm around her, hugging her. "He's a lot closer here than if he was still back in North Carolina so…"

"I know, I know. There's just been a lot of changes here lately and…I guess I'm trying to figure out what's next."

Building a house they'd designed had taken longer than originally planned and they had to do work on the cabin simultaneously to make it a little more habitable for them. It meant they were surrounded by construction for a good part of the time. On top of that, Josiah had been re-elected as the sheriff of Silver Bell Falls and Melanie had written and published two books. Life had been moving at a pretty hectic pace. They'd been working so hard to be exactly where they were right now that Melanie wasn't sure what she was supposed to do with herself.

"Funny you should mention that," Josiah said smoothly, pulling back just a bit so he could see her face. "I've been giving it a lot of thought."

"Really?"

He nodded. "Really." Then, taking her hand in his, he touched the vintage style engagement ring Melanie wore. When his eyes met hers, they were so full of tenderness that Melanie's heart seriously skipped a beat. "The election, your deadlines, and this house have consumed us for almost two years now."

Swallowing hard, she said, "I know."

"And we both agreed that when I put this ring on your finger, we weren't going to rush into making wedding plans because it would make us both crazy."

She nodded. "I remember." And she had to keep from complimenting herself on how calm she sounded because now that she realized where this conversation was heading, she felt incredibly nervous.

There wasn't a doubt in her mind that she wanted to marry Josiah Stone. He had been her only beacon of hope at a time when she felt so completely lost and alone. The thought of spending the rest of her life with him excited her.

Except…now that they were most likely going

to start planning the rest of their lives, that excitement was making her feel a little sick.

In a good way!

Slowly, she let out a breath and waited for Josiah to continue.

"So I'd like to think that we can start talking about this without making ourselves crazy." The slow and sexy grin he gave her helped calm her nerves a little. She wanted to marry Josiah more than anything in the world and he was right—they were finally at a place where their lives had calmed down. It truly was the best time to start talking about wedding plans.

"I agree," she said softly, squeezing his hand. "Where do we even begin?"

"Actually, I may have undersold myself when I said I've been giving this a lot of thought."

She looked at him in confusion. "What does that even mean?"

Twisting in his spot, he faced her head on. "Mel, I am a planner. It's just in my nature and I can't help it."

The nervous laugh that came out couldn't be stopped. "I know that and it's one of the things I love about you!"

"I know I can be overwhelming at times because you're much more laid back in how you do things," he explained, and Melanie felt like this was simply a stalling tactic.

"Okay, so you've got some concrete ideas about our wedding," she stated evenly. "That's great! So…come on. Talk to me. What have you thought about? What kind of wedding do you see us having?"

It was the long breath he let out that gave Melanie her first clue that she wasn't going to like what he had planned.

And the statement he blurted out confirmed it.

"I want us to have a Christmas wedding."

"What?" she cried.

Josiah knew he was taking a big risk in presenting this to her—after all, Melanie had grown up hating Christmas. Hell, he'd only gotten her to have some good feelings toward the holiday in the last two years! But he knew if she'd just give him a chance, he'd be able to prove to her how a Christmas wedding would be amazing.

Jumping to his feet, he looked down at her shocked expression and did his best to keep his tone light and encouraging.

"Just…hear me out, okay?"

The look on her face said she would, but she certainly wasn't happy about it.

"What could be better than getting married during such a festive time of the year?" he began but didn't give her a chance to reply. "Think about it—everything, everywhere is already beautifully decorated. Any place we go won't require much from us because it will already be decorated! The Poinsettias, Christmas trees, the lights…all that work will be done for us."

"Josiah…"

"And everyone will be in town already so there won't be a need for them to make a separate trip."

"Who's everyone? My dad is already here; he's the only family I have and your family doesn't live that far away. It's hardly like they'd be making a huge sacrifice to come to town," she countered.

"But all of our friends will be here too. You know how most people we know tend to travel either before Christmas or after the new year because they love all the festivities here in town Christmas week."

Melanie let out a small sigh. "Look, I get what you're saying. I really do. But…you know my feelings on Christmas."

He immediately sat back down at her side. "And we've come such a long way, Mel! When we first met, you hated the holidays and everything about them. But after that first Christmas here, you changed. You saw how it all wasn't so bad and—admit it—you even enjoyed it."

She gave him a sour look. "I know that first Christmas was amazing but only because you made it that way for me. You went out of your way to make up for every single crappy Christmas I'd had since I was five!"

"And what about last year?" he prodded.

Another sigh. "You proposed last Christmas so of course that's going to make for a great memory."

"So you see…"

"But," she quickly interrupted, "that doesn't mean I want to get married during the month of December or anywhere near Christmas!"

He silently admitted to himself that he knew

there were going to be some challenges in getting Melanie to see his way of thinking, but he was kind of hopeful that she wouldn't be quite this hostile toward the idea. How was he supposed to convince her that this could be good for them? Great, even? What could he possibly do to show her how wonderful a Christmas wedding could be?

So he decided to opt for another tactic.

"Okay then… tell me when you think we should get married."

Melanie's eyes went wide. "Me?"

He nodded. "I told you what I was thinking and now it's your turn to tell me your thoughts."

"But…I haven't thought about it!"

"Mel, you can't tell me you haven't—not once—thought about our wedding. It's not possible."

"Fine," she murmured. "I guess when I thought about our wedding, I envisioned it as being warmer weather. Outdoors. And a bit…rustic."

Now they were getting somewhere.

"Rustic, huh? I like that idea," he said.

"Really?" she asked, excitedly.

"Absolutely! I think we could look into renting out the barn Hank and Lisa built off of Old Main Street. They've used it for a lot of events in the past. What do you think?"

Then her eyes lit up because they were clearly on the same page. "That's what I thought too! I mean…the few times when I thought about it," she added. "When we went to the Valentine's Day dance there last year, I remember thinking how wonderful it was and how I really liked the rustic look."

Nodding, he took her hand in his. "And I think we can make it look incredible for a wedding."

"I think so too!" And then she was in his arms and kissing him. And not that he was complaining but…this was only one small detail and they had many, many bigger ones to deal with.

But kissing Melanie was slightly addictive and he figured that maybe—just maybe—they could take a few minutes and simply enjoy each other before they dealt with any more wedding plans.

Melanie, however, wasn't so inclined.

Lifting her head, she looked at him giddily. "So then we agree—the barn in the spring and it will be perfect and…"

"Wait, wait, wait," Josiah said, putting some distance between them. "I'm not on board with the spring. I still want us to have a Christmas wedding."

"Josiah, be reasonable. Please."

That wasn't quite what he was expecting her to say. "I don't think I'm being unreasonable here. I tossed out a date, you tossed out a date, and now we…you know…negotiate."

Crossing her arms over her chest she eyed him warily. "And are you going to counter every date I suggest with Christmas?"

Busted!

"Possibly."

She rolled her eyes. "Then what's the point? If you're not going to give on this, then how is that fair?"

"Melanie…"

"And," she interrupted again, "might I remind you of how you always do this to me?"

"Do what?" he demanded. "We've never tried to plan our wedding before!"

"Not the wedding, but everything else Christmas-related!"

Now he was totally confused. "What are you talking about?"

"Do you remember the parade?"

It would have been foolish to play dumb. He had totally manipulated her for her own good to get her to participate in the Silver Bell Falls Annual Christmas Parade when she first came to town.

"And how you got me to put up a Christmas tree in the cabin because you didn't have room in the tiny house?"

"Well, in all fairness…"

"And then there was the tree shopping and picking out ornaments and…"

"Okay, okay…I get what you're saying," he confessed. "But you have to admit that even though you thought you didn't want to do those things, you ended up enjoying yourself!"

"It's still manipulation, Josiah," she argued. "You suggest something, I say no and then you come up with some sort of crazy reasoning and in the end, you get your way! How is that fair?"

Unfortunately, she had him there. He'd always known that he did find ways around her objections to anything Christmas-related, but he also knew it always worked out and Melanie was happy. And he knew if she would just give him a chance, he could get her to come around to his way of thinking and their wedding would be beyond her wildest dreams.

Now it was time to time to go big or go home.

"How about this," he said evenly. "Let's make an appointment to go and see the barn decorated for Christmas. I know I can call Lisa and she can set it up so you can get an idea of how it will all look."

"It's not about the decorations, Josiah…"

"And if you don't like it," he went on as if she hadn't objected, "then I promise to be more open-minded about another date."

Melanie eyed him warily again. And with good reason, he imagined.

"What do you say, Mel? I can make the call and next weekend we can go and look and make some decisions."

Her shoulders sagged slightly. "I guess it can't hurt," she murmured. "But I don't see what the big rush is. Why not just wait until she gets the decorations up? Even if I agree to this crazy idea, we have a whole year to plan."

Now it was his turn to be confused. "A whole year? Um…Mel? I was talking about us getting married this year. This Christmas."

# Chapter Two

A week later and Melanie was still fuming. Inwardly mostly, but fuming nonetheless.

"There's Lisa," Josiah said. The drive to the barn had been spent in relative silence—as had much of their week. He looked over at her with a small smile. "Ready?"

"Yup." Honestly, she was more than a little curious about how the barn was going to look when it was all decorated, but she was still peeved that Josiah couldn't understand why it was such a big deal to her to try to plan a wedding in less than two months and at Christmas! It didn't matter how much they talked about it this week—when they were talking—Josiah was still overly optimistic that they could pull off their dream wedding on such short notice. If time were their only issue, she could have possibly been on board. The time of year was her biggest hang-up.

She climbed from their car and met him at the hood. When he took one of her hands in his and gently squeezed it, Melanie couldn't help but smile. They'd get through this. Surely they'd talk to Lisa and she'd tell them it was impossible to pull off a wedding on such short notice. The place was obviously here, but there were so many other things to consider—invitations, caterer, music, her dress...

Melanie gasped loudly.

"What?" Josiah asked nervously. "What's the matter?"

Why hadn't she thought about this before? Why hadn't either of them thought about this in all their short discussions this week?

Tears stung her eyes and she wanted to curse them. This wasn't a bad thing; it was a good thing! This was the exact detail she needed to get her out of this Christmas wedding and to prove how they needed more time to plan!

"A dress!" she cried. "Josiah, I don't have a dress!"

He looked at her oddly. "So? We can go buy one. I don't see what the big deal is."

She rolled her eyes. "You cannot just go out and buy a wedding gown. They have to be ordered and then fitted and that takes months. Months!"

He must have thought this was just a made-up excuse, because he wasn't the least bit flustered by her announcement. "We'll talk about that later. Right now, Lisa's waiting for us."

"But..."

Raising her hand to his lips, he kissed it.

"Come on. Let's go see how the barn looks."

It was pointless to argue and really, the curiosity was starting to kill her.

Together they walked toward the barn and greeted Lisa.

"Hey, you two! I'm so glad you could make it," Lisa said. She was a native to Silver Bell Falls and she and her husband Hank were known for their handmade wood ornaments. They sold them every year at the big craft sale that was held right after the Christmas parade. The very first ornament Melanie had ever purchased was from Hank and Lisa.

"Thanks for doing this on such notice," Josiah said with a smile. "I hope it wasn't too much trouble."

Lisa waved him off with a smile of her own. "It wasn't a big deal at all. I love seeing this place decorated for the holidays and I was probably going to do it in another week or two so really, you just helped me get an early start." Then she looked at Melanie and her smile grew. "You are going to love what we've done in here."

"Oh?"

Stepping closer to the doors, Lisa explained. "We've had holiday parties here in the past and have kept to the basics of decor—lights, wreaths, and trees—but what I went for this time around, was a little more of a..." she looked over her shoulder at the two of them with a hint of giddiness. "Winter Wonderland."

She swung the double-doors open and motioned for them to step inside. There was some snow on the ground outside and as Melanie and

Josiah stepped into the barn, it almost felt the same inside.

Releasing Josiah's hand, Melanie stepped into the large open space in awe. There were white twinkly lights and tiny silver stars hanging from the ceiling which gave the impression of a night sky. There were also two massive white chandeliers there that she'd never seen before. They had garland and red bows woven through them. Around the room were several tall and beautifully decorated Christmas trees and in between them were birch trees lit up with white lights. And the tables…the settings were everything Melanie could ever imagine and more.

"Lisa," she said with wonder. "You have really outdone yourself. I…I can't believe you accomplished all of this in a week!"

Appreciative of the praise, Lisa blushed. "As much as I love that you think I was able to pull this together so quickly, the truth is I've been working on this stuff for about six months."

"Um…excuse me?" Melanie asked as she glanced at Josiah, silently accusing him of somehow orchestrating this for so long.

"Last Christmas we had several parties here and everything looked fine," Lisa explained, "but I knew we could do more. So I've been scouring Pinterest for some new ideas." She walked over to one of the tables. "Let me explain what we have here—and know that I do have a few other options if you don't like what you see."

It was on the tip of Melanie's tongue to tell her how she didn't have to explain anything. Without a wedding gown, there was no way they could get married this Christmas. Next Christmas? Maybe. The more she looked around the room, the more she could easily picture herself getting married in this setting. But right now...

"You'll notice that each place setting has one of these silver pinecones," she said as she held one up. "These frosty-looking pinecones are the classic winter adornment. Scatter them about your wedding for an instant - and cost-effective -seasonal touch. We put place cards in the top of them so your guests have a festive way of seeing where they sit."

"Those are precious," Melanie murmured and beside her, Josiah agreed.

"Josiah told me you wanted a rustic theme, so I did my best to combine that with a holiday feel. We can add more reds if you'd like, but I went with the white, silver and gold tablescape. I wanted to create a festive feel with clever and creative tablescaping; cinnamon sticks, pinecones, log slices and fir foliage all create a woodland ambiance." She looked at both of them and smiled. "I believe this—along with the barn atmosphere—really work well together."

Neither of them could argue with her logic.

"And look at the cloth napkins!" Lisa added. "I combined cinnamon sticks and winter berries, for a chic and organic napkin ring alternative. Aren't they perfect?"

If Melanie didn't put a stop to this now, she'd get so wrapped up in Lisa's excitement that she'd be willing to get married in yoga pants and a sweatshirt!

"Now I have to admit, Hank is responsible for the chairs," Lisa said as she pulled one of the chairs from the table. "Fussy chair covers wouldn't really work in this environment. But I didn't want to just leave them bare. While Hank was trimming the trees, he hung some of the discarded branches over the chair and I saw them and thought…perfect! So, a little greenery and some red velvet ribbon and—voila! —we have something more rustic and simple."

"I never would have thought of that," Josiah said and Melanie wanted to remind him how decorating on any level wasn't his thing. When they had shopped for furniture for their new house, she had to stop him from picking everything that was brown and leather and functional. Functional was fine, but he had no creativity—or any idea how women preferred color and style in their homes.

Lisa moved toward the center of the room and pointed up at the ceiling. "These chandeliers are big and beautiful but they don't throw off an excessive amount of light. Combined with the twinkly lights, I think we can create a really cozy atmosphere at your wedding reception. It will really feel like an outdoor event combined with the low lighting, lots of candles and a touch of sparkle."

"It really does feel…magical in here, doesn't it, Mel?" Josiah asked.

She was about to answer when she noticed something unusual in the corner of the room. "Um…what's that?"

"Ooo…that is going to be the highlight of

every party this winter!" Lisa exclaimed as she walked across the room. "This is a hot chocolate bar!"

"A hot chocolate bar?" both Melanie and Josiah repeated.

"Uh-huh! Isn't it fabulous?"

"It's…it's…"

"Actually, we're calling it a cocoa bar, but we're going to serve mulled wine and hot brandy cocktails too! It's a wonderful alternative to your standard bar and with the cold weather, guests will appreciate coming inside and having something hot to drink. Of course, you can serve whatever you want, but this is an option for you if you're interested."

"You keep speaking as if you're handling the food, beverages and…pretty much everything," Josiah commented. "I thought you just rented out the space and then someone else catered and decorated and handled the rest."

"That was how we used to do things," she explained. "And anyone who rents the space is more than welcome to bring in their own people. But…you know what a close-knit town we are and there aren't a lot of spaces available for big parties other than the churches, so the more events we had here, the more I got to work with party planners and caterers—all of whom are local—and it just seemed like a smart thing to start working together. You know, professionally."

"So…now you're in the party planning business?" Melanie asked, a bit wide-eyed and surprised at the announcement. "But what about the ornaments and Hank's wood carving business?"

She waved them off. "Hank's relieved to have me doing this so I'm out of his hair a bit more," she said with a laugh. "I love working with him, but I found I loved working solo and being able to express my own creativity a lot more!"

"That's amazing!" Josiah said. "And your love of what you do really shows. This place truly is a winter wonderland! We love it, don't we, Mel?"

There was no way she could lie. "It really is amazing in here, Lisa. And if I had a gown, I know I'd be tempted to book you right now, but..."

"You need a gown?" Lisa asked, sounding more excited than worried.

"Yes, she does!" Josiah answered before Melanie could.

Rubbing her hands together, Lisa's eyes lit up. "Well, it just so happens that my niece Jessica got engaged last month and they are planning a wedding for Thanksgiving weekend—a short timeline like yours!"

"Oh, um...we're still not..." Melanie tried to explain but Lisa was talking again.

"I got to go dress shopping with her and Marie—my sister—in New York City two weeks ago and she found a fabulous dress right off the rack at one of those sample boutiques!"

"Sample boutique? What's that?" Melanie asked, mildly intrigued.

"Apparently, several top bridal salons, showrooms and manufacturers have been opening discrete sample stores where they can divest themselves of extra inventory and where a bride-to-be can walk out with a deeply-discounted gown, ready for final alterations by her own tailor! Amazing, right? I remember when you had to order your gown six months before the wedding!"

"Is that so?" Josiah asked as he grinned at Melanie. "And right there in New York City? Sounds like a great excuse for a weekend trip!"

"Oh, it was," Lisa said. "It was. We had a fabulous time and none of them take appointments—you just walk in and shop. I'm telling you, Melanie, they had every style of gown imaginable!"

Great. There went her gown excuse.

"I can get the list of all the shops we went to and email it to you," she continued. "Marie's a list-maker by nature and I know she'll have those names handy for anyone who needs them."

"Thanks, Lisa," she said, smiling stiffly.

"So what else can I do for the two of you?"

It wasn't as if he was going to do a victory dance just yet, but there wasn't a doubt in his mind that after seeing the barn and hearing of all the options for getting a wedding gown, Melanie would agree to getting married for Christmas.

The drive back to the house had been almost as quiet as the one to the barn. He knew when to hold his tongue and let Melanie think things through.

This was one of those times.

But the suspense was killing him. There were

several times while they were walking around the barn when he saw the excitement in her eyes and how much she loved what she was seeing. He also knew she could be stubborn and would need time to reason it all out in her head before agreeing to anything.

"How about Italian for dinner tonight?" he asked as they walked into the house. "I think I can whip up a quick Bolognese sauce if you're interested."

Melanie shrugged.

He made his way to the kitchen, pulled open the refrigerator and scanned the contents. "We can have a salad and garlic bread with it too."

"Uh-huh…"

Okay, he'd hit his limit. For the last week he had done his best not to push his agenda on her, but he was getting tired of their stilted conversations. From the moment Melanie Harper had walked into his life, they'd had great chemistry, great banter and could talk for hours on end about everything and nothing at all. He missed that. And especially now when they were in their new home and should be happy and celebrating, he hated how things were strained between them.

And whose fault is that?

Yeah, okay, that one was totally on him. Josiah knew he wasn't being reasonable about the wedding. After all, it wasn't like they had to get married this Christmas. He just wanted to. If it had been up to him, he would have married Melanie that very first Christmas they were together—and they had only known each other for less than eight weeks! She was it for him.

Those light blue eyes, her long dark hair, her smile, her laugh…even her stubbornness all made her who she was and he loved her. He wanted to spend the rest of his life with her and wanted that life to start as soon as possible.

Closing the refrigerator door, Josiah walked across the room to where Melanie was sitting at their kitchen table looking at something on her phone. Without a word, he reached down and carefully pulled her to her feet.

She didn't say anything—not out loud—but her eyes scanned his face and he read all of her questions there.

Slowly, he pulled her into his arms and rested his forehead against hers. "Hey," he said softly.

A small smile pulled at her lips. "Hey yourself."

"I've missed you."

With a slight head tilt, she studied him. "I'm right here."

"I know but…I feel like we've both been a little distant this week and…I hate it. I envisioned our first week in the house being much different."

"Oh really," she said as she pressed a little closer. "How so?"

"For starters, I envisioned us talking a lot more," he explained. "And laughing. And having a lot more sex."

That last one had her laughing quietly. "I'll tell you what…"

He instantly perked up.

"How about you give me a few minutes head

start and I'll go draw a bath…"

"Go on…"

"And I'll add lots of bubbles…"

"Uh-huh…"

"And you can join me and we'll work on crossing all those things off your list, Sheriff. What do you say?"

His entire body seemed to harden. "I say I'm glad we got a tub big enough for two!"

# Chapter Three

The next morning, they were lying in bed and Melanie knew last night had been the perfect—and sexiest—distraction for them, but they needed to talk about the elephant in the room.

Snuggled up beside him under the blankets, she kissed his chest before resting her head back on his shoulder. "We need to talk."

His arm tightened around her and she felt a light kiss on the top of her head. "I know."

Confrontation in any form was something Melanie tended to shy away from as much as possible, but this was important and as uncomfortable as she knew it could be, it still had to be dealt with.

So many thoughts tumbled around in her head and yet she couldn't seem to organize them enough to speak. Luckily Josiah seemed to sense that and spoke first.

"Mel, we took a long time to plan and build this house and it's everything we ever wanted, right?"

She nodded.

"We talked endlessly about the things we wanted and the details that were important to us. We looked at magazines and websites and watched home shows to get ideas and in the end, we were able to incorporate all the features that we had to have, right?"

She nodded again but had no idea where he was going with this.

"But once we knew what we wanted, it all came together pretty quickly, didn't it? The hardest part was sitting down and talking through our ideas and the things we thought were important. After that, everything else fell into place."

"It still took almost eighteen months from start to finish," she reminded him. "The house wasn't built overnight."

"I know, I know, but a lot of the delays were weather-related. If you took that out, the timeline was much shorter, wasn't it?"

"I suppose."

"When you write your books, how long does it typically take you?"

"It depends," she said softly. "Some stories just come to me and they flow effortlessly. I've written a novel in a month, but most of the time it takes two to three."

"It's a little like the house planning," he went on. "Once everything is worked out in your mind, the rest just seems to flow."

"Josiah, what exactly are you trying to say? It's too early for my brain to be following the way this conversation is going back and forth between houses and books."

He chuckled softly and placed another kiss on top of her head. "Mel, we already know we want to get married. We have the place and it's decorated beautifully. We've been living together almost since we met. I don't think we need to wait another year for a wedding. Personally, I don't want to wait that long." Then he shifted so he could look at her face and smiled softly. "I want you to be my wife. The sooner the better."

Her heart kicked hard in her chest and that's when it hit her.

She wanted to be his wife sooner rather than later too. Waiting another year just meant obsessing about things for a longer period of time.

"I don't want to wait another year either," she began carefully. "I love you and I want to be your wife, but…can't we at least talk about another date? Something that doesn't have to do with the holidays?" And before he could comment, she quickly added, "Wouldn't it be nice to have a date that is just ours? Something we aren't sharing with the rest of the world?"

He sighed and she knew he was disappointed. Truth be known, she hated to be the one to make him feel that way, but she also knew she'd feel worse if she kept her feelings to herself. This was going to be their wedding and it should be on both of their terms.

The silence was beginning to make Melanie

nervous, so she looked up. "Josiah?"

Another sigh. "I get what you're saying and I guess I thought we had crossed that hurdle and you were over your whole hating of all-things-Christmas." He shrugged. "In my head, I thought it would be the perfect way for you to have a whole different view of it—something positive and happy to wash away all the negative memories."

Rolling over, she placed her hand on his chest directly over his heart. "You have done so much to make that happen and I really have learned that not everything about Christmas is bad, but…it doesn't mean I want to share the happiest day of my life with it. Think about it, Josiah. As magical as it all sounds in your head, think of the reality of having it as our anniversary. We'd never get to celebrate it on its own—it's always going to be a holiday to celebrate something else. And when we have kids, our anniversary will get lost in the shuffle. Is that really what you want?"

By the look on his face, he hadn't thought about these things. Melanie knew how much Josiah loved Christmas and everything about it. Living his entire life in Silver Bell Falls, how could he not? It was like living in a giant Christmas card year-round! That's why she felt it was important for him to be open to looking at other dates. While she could completely concede that Christmas and everything that went with it could be wonderful, there were also a lot of other wonderful times of the year for them to consider.

"How about this," she began, hoping to encourage him a bit. "Let's go and have some breakfast, break out the calendar and start looking at it. How does that sound?"

He considered her for a long moment. "Do you mind if I take a shower first?"

Not quite the response she was looking for but… "Sure! I'll go get out all the makings for pancakes and get them started. Sound good?" She knew pancakes were one of his favorite breakfast foods and she hoped it would work in her favor by putting him in a good mood while they talked about potential non-Christmas dates.

Just as she was about to move away from him, Josiah surprised her by wrapping her in his arms and twisting them until she was beneath him. He kissed her thoroughly, deeply and left her completely breathless.

"Wow," she said, trying to catch her breath. "The thought of pancakes got you that worked up?"

He laughed softly. "No. The thought of marrying you did."

Winding her arms around him, Melanie hugged him close. "Breakfast can wait a little while longer, right?"

And by the sexy grin on his face, Josiah completely agreed.

Josiah waited until Melanie was out of the bedroom and he heard her working in the kitchen before moving from the bed. The first thing he did was reach for his phone and tap out a quick text for reinforcements. He wasn't quite ready to admit defeat on his wedding plans and he knew he was going to need a little help if he was going to have a chance.

Placing his phone back down on the nightstand, he walked into the bathroom and took his shower. As he luxuriated in the large, tiled space, he couldn't help but remember all the times he had dreamed of this—not just living with Melanie, but having a shower that was big enough for him. The time he spent living in his tiny house before moving into the cabin with Melanie had been met with several challenges.

The shower being the biggest, ironically.

So to have a spa-quality bathroom with a shower not only big enough for him, but big enough to fit several people? Yeah, this was like a dream come true. And if he wasn't careful, he'd spend way too much time in here and he needed to get to Melanie and their breakfast before his wedding helper and co-conspirator arrived.

Shutting off the water, he quickly toweled off and got dressed. By the time he walked into the kitchen, he was surprised to find the table set, coffee made and a platter of pancakes waiting for him on the table.

He let out a soft laugh. "How long was I up there?"

Melanie turned to him with a knowing grin. "I can see that shower is going to be an issue. Should I be jealous?"

He took the teasing as it was meant. "I can't help it. It's glorious."

"That we can agree on," she said lightly as she plated up some sizzling bacon for them.

"Bacon too?" he asked with surprise. "I must have been very good this morning." He went to grab a slice, but she swatted his hand away. "Ow!"

"Stop. I had to make a little extra. My dad called and is stopping by. I wanted to make sure we had enough food."

There were enough pancakes on the table to feed a small army, he thought, but kept it to himself. "How come John's coming over? Is everything okay?"

As if on cue, the doorbell rang. Josiah stayed in the kitchen and poured himself a cup of coffee while Melanie ran to let her father in. He heard their greetings and hid his smile behind his coffee mug when they both walked into the kitchen.

"Hey, Josiah," John said as he came over and shook his hand. "Hope you don't mind me barging in on your breakfast."

"You know you're welcome here any time," Josiah replied smoothly and then motioned to the pot of coffee. "Help yourself."

"Thanks."

"You were a little cryptic on the phone, Dad," Melanie chimed in. "What's going on?"

The three of them sat down at the table and began helping themselves to the food.

"I'm struggling with the plans for the house," John said, cutting into his stack of pancakes. "I have loved living in the tiny house, but—similar to the issues Josiah had—I definitely need more space to do the things I want to do."

"Like what?" Melanie asked, looking mildly confused.

"I want to be able to have a Christmas tree," he said casually. "I remember Josiah telling me about how he hadn't thought about that when he purchased the house and how he had to decorate the cabin that first Christmas in order to use his decorations."

"So you're designing your new home based on a tree?" Melanie deadpanned.

Both John and Josiah chuckled. "It's not just that," John explained. "And it's not like I'm talking about a lot of extra space, but definitely more than I have now." He took a sip of his coffee. "I'm going to want at least two guest rooms for when you two have kids, which I'm hoping is going to be soon. I'm not getting any younger, you know."

Josiah merrily bit into a slice of bacon as he watched Melanie's eyes go wide.

"Dad, we haven't started talking about kids. We're not even married yet!"

John placed his fork down and looked at his daughter. "And that's something else I wanted to talk to you about. The two of you have been engaged for almost a year now. Don't you think it's time you set a date?"

"Funny you should mention that, John," Josiah said, "because Melanie and I have been talking about it this past week."

"Excellent! Oh, that's good news! So…when's the big day?" John asked anxiously.

Josiah looked across the table at Melanie, who was still sitting there wide-eyed.

"Uh...well..." Melanie began.

"Actually, John, we're not quite in agreement on that yet," Josiah jumped in to explain. "Just this morning we agreed to pull out the calendar to try to decide."

John looked between the two of them and smiled. "Mind if I help?"

"Dad, I don't think you want to..."

"Mel, your dad could be the exact thing we need to help us make our decision. He's an objective third party," Josiah reasoned.

"I guess." But she didn't look completely convinced.

They ate in silence for a few minutes before John asked them to catch him up on what they were thinking in terms of wedding dates. Josiah went first and laid out his plans for a Christmas wedding—including everything they had seen the previous day with Hank and Lisa's barn and how so many of the details were already taken care of since Lisa had the barn ready.

"Wow," John said, nodding. "It sounds amazing." Then he looked at Melanie. "And you didn't like it?"

She shook her head. "That's not it at all. I loved it. Everything was beautiful."

"Then...what's the problem?"

First she shot Josiah a glare, then she looked at her father. "Isn't it enough that I have settled down in Christmastown, USA? Do I really have to share my wedding day with the holiday too?"

"I thought you were over that," John replied. "You know, your aversion to Christmas."

With a loud huff of frustration, Melanie stood and walked across the kitchen to refresh her coffee. "This isn't only about that!" she cried. "As the bride, aren't I entitled to have what I want on my wedding day?"

In that moment, Josiah felt a little guilty. "Mel, maybe we should…"

She held up a hand to stop him. "No, you wanted to get an impartial third-party opinion on this, so he deserves to have all the facts." Then she turned to her father and explained how she had envisioned her wedding—which basically was almost identical to what Josiah wanted, just minus the holiday cheer.

When she was done talking, she sat back down and pushed her food around on her plate.

John reached over and covered one of her hands with his. "Okay, planning a wedding isn't supposed to stress people out until you are well underway. This is too much too soon," he commented.

And as Josiah sat there and watched Melanie looking so miserable, he knew what he had to do. Slowly, he pushed his plate away and reached over and took the fork out of her hand before clasping her hand in his. "I didn't mean to put this much pressure on you. I guess I thought you'd warm up to the idea just like you have with all the other holiday-related things I've thrown your way. I was being selfish and I'm sorry."

When she looked up at him, her eyes were wet with unshed tears. "All of those things did end up being better than I thought, but…this isn't a parade or a tree, Josiah. This is going to be one of the biggest days of our lives."

He swallowed hard. "I know," he said quietly. "I know."

"So where does that leave us?" she asked, emotion clogging her throat.

"It leaves us looking at dates on the calendar after January first." The words almost stuck in his throat, but he said them and he meant them. As much as having a Christmas wedding meant to him, Melanie meant more. The last thing he wanted was for them to start out their lives together with hard feelings about their wedding and him not playing fair to get his way.

Looking at John, he nodded.

"Are you sure you're okay with this?" Melanie asked.

At the moment, no, but he opted to keep that to himself. "I am. I want us to have the perfect wedding and that means on a date we both agree on, okay?"

She visibly relaxed and just like that, it was like a switch flipped. Melanie began to talk excitedly about how she could see them using most of Lisa's décor at the barn and modifying them to look a little less wintery and how she could still use the referrals for wedding boutiques in New York City because she didn't want to have to plan their wedding around how long it took to get her gown.

"This is so exciting!" she said, jumping up from her chair. "I'm going to go grab my laptop so we can start looking at the calendar!" She gave Josiah a loud smacking kiss on his cheek before sprinting from the room.

When she was out of sight, John looked at him. "You're a good man, Josiah."

He shrugged. "Her happiness means more to me than anything. And she's right. I've pushed my own agenda regarding the holidays since we met. It's time for me to respect her boundaries—especially on such an important day."

"I know how much this meant to you and I was more than willing to come here today and try to persuade Melanie to be a little more open-minded. I guess—like you—I didn't realize how much this sort of thing still bothered her."

Josiah was about to comment but his cell phone rang. Pulling it from his pocket, he glanced at the screen and quickly answered. He listened as his deputy gave him the details of a high-speed chase heading toward the city limits of Silver Bell.

"I'm on my way," he said firmly and slipped his phone back into his pocket.

"Everything okay?" John asked, coming to his feet as Josiah did.

"Looks like a bit of trouble is heading toward town in the form of a chase. I need to get out there and see what we can do to slow it down and maybe stop things before someone gets hurt." He moved around the kitchen with efficiency as he grabbed his shoes and his coat. Walking to the mudroom, he crouched down and opened the safe where he kept his gun, badge, and holster.

Melanie walked in just then. "What's going on?"

He straightened and kissed her on the cheek.

"We've got a chase heading toward town. I've got to go and do my thing." He kissed her one more time. "I love you."

"I love you too," she said, worry lacing her features.

There wasn't time to say more. The drive into town would take fifteen minutes and he'd be on the line the entire time with his team to make sure the area was secured. Adrenaline began to pump as he got his head into sheriff mode.

And as he pulled away from the house, wedding dates were the last thing on his mind. Keeping the people of Silver Bell Falls safe was his only concern.

# Chapter Four

Later that afternoon, Melanie was sitting at her desk and working on her next book. She had a huge picture window in front of her that gave her a fantastic view of the property and she smiled as she looked up and saw a little bit of snow starting to fall. She shivered slightly and her mind wandered to what she was going to make for dinner tonight. It seemed like the perfect weather for some homemade soup or stew, but she wasn't sure there was enough time to make one.

Standing, she stretched and walked down the hall to the kitchen to see what kind of ingredients she had on hand. Josiah tended to do the grocery shopping—something he loved but she hated—and every day became a game of "What's for dinner?" She was about to pull the refrigerator door open when the doorbell began to ring incessantly.

"What in the world?" she murmured, walking quickly toward the door. Pulling open the door, she gasped when she saw her father standing there looking solemn. "Dad? What are you…?"

He stepped inside and gently grasped her shoulders. "Mel, has anyone called you yet?"

She didn't need to ask why. Her heart simply stopped. This was the moment she always dreaded every time Josiah walked out the door. Her eyes instantly began to sting with tears as she shook her head. "What happened? Where is he?"

"Go get your coat," he said, his voice a little gruff. "They took him to Silver Bell Memorial."

Grabbing her purse, she followed her father out of the house and climbed into his car, which was still running. They hadn't even made it off the property when she began grilling him for information.

"Did someone call you? Why didn't they call me?" Digging through her purse, she pulled out her phone. "Who do I need to call? Is anyone at the station?"

"Mel, you have to calm down, sweetheart."

"Calm down? Dad, you tell me something's happened to Josiah but you haven't said what. You tell me he's at the hospital, but you won't say why! You need to tell me what's going on!"

"From what I can tell—and mind you, this is largely hearsay because I wasn't there myself and you know how gossip flies around town and…"

"Dad!" she cried with frustration. "Focus!"

John let out a slow breath. "Okay, I went into town to grab some lunch and a lot of the roads were still blocked off. I thought it was a little odd since Josiah had left right after breakfast. So I was in the diner and everyone was talking about it." He paused. "Normally you only see a crowd like that at breakfast, but it was wall-to-wall people in there."

"Dad..." Melanie prompted with annoyance.

"The chase coming through town originated in Albany. The guy being chased is wanted for a double-homicide and had already caused multiple accidents."

"Oh my gosh..."

"The way law enforcement figured, the guy should have been running out of gas by the time he hit our city limits. There were roadblocks set up all over town—Josiah was at the last one."

With her stomach in knots, she both needed to know and dreaded what she was about to hear. "What happened?"

"Mel..."

"I need to know, Dad!"

"The driver crashed through the first three and everyone knew he was going to do the same at the last one. They don't have any major deterrents to stop drivers—at the first three they used construction barrels and several cars but that did little more than slow this guy down momentarily. His car was damaged but he didn't stop."

John paused and Melanie wanted to scream with frustration.

"Josiah had less at his disposal because no one expected the driver to get that far so essentially..."

"It was just him," she said quietly.

"He shot out the front tire and the driver went off the road and hit a tree. Josiah went to confront him and was shot."

Crying out in horror, Melanie felt like she was going to be sick.

"Where...I mean...what...what happened next?"

"There was already a line of law enforcement on this guy's tail so they got there just as it happened. They were able to apprehend the guy and get an ambulance to Josiah as fast as they could."

Her heart was in her throat at the image of Josiah fighting for his life! "Dad, what else do you know? How was he when the paramedics got to him?"

"All I know, Mel, was he was shot and unconscious. Someone said he was shot twice but...I don't know for sure." Taking one hand from the steering wheel, John reached over and took his daughter's hand. "I wish I knew more. I really do."

Tears were streaming down her face and she cursed the long drive to the hospital. "Should I call the hospital? The station? I...I just don't know what to do and I feel so helpless!"

"You can try to call the hospital, but we'll be there soon enough. You do whatever you need to do to put your mind at ease."

Somehow, Melanie didn't think anything was going to put her mind to ease except seeing Josiah for herself and hearing that he was going to be all right. But in the meantime, she placed a call to the hospital. After a bit of a runaround, the only information she was given was how he was indeed in the emergency room and the doctors were with him. With a curse, she made her next call to the station and got one of the deputies—Jared O'Neil.

"Jared, it's Melanie," she said quickly. "Do you have any updates on Josiah?"

"I wish we did, Melanie, and I'm sorry. Things are a bit out of control here right now. I believe Drew Maxwell—he's new to the force—is at the hospital with him. I'll text you his number right now and you can call him."

"Thanks, Jared." She hung up and thankfully his text came through a minute later.

"We're almost there, Mel," her father said and as she looked around, she knew it would still be at least another ten minutes before they pulled up to the small hospital.

With little more than a nod, she quickly tried calling Drew's number but it went directly to voicemail.

"For all you know, he's on the line updating them at the station," John said calmly.

The rest of the drive was spent in silence and Melanie was relieved when her father dropped her off in front of the ER so she could go right in while he parked the car.

Running to the front desk, she did her best to calmly ask to see Josiah.

"Are you family?" the receptionist asked.

"I'm his fiancée," she said and looked around for anyone she knew who might be able to give her information faster than the staff would.

"Miss Harper?"

Turning, Melanie saw a deputy walking toward her. She didn't recognize him and hoped it was Drew Maxwell. A quick glimpse at his badge confirmed it. "I just tried calling you," she said, shaking his hand. "Any updates on Josiah?"

He shook his head. "I'm sorry. The last update I got was that they were taking him for x-rays."

"Miss Harper?"

This time she turned back to the receptionist. "Yes?"

"You can go back now." There was a nurse in a pair of scrubs standing behind the desk and she gave Melanie a small smile.

When she looked at Drew, she spotted her father walking in. "They're letting me go see Josiah. I'll be back out as soon as I can," she said before following the nurse back.

They went through the first set of doors before Melanie asked, "Is he awake? Will I be able to talk to him?"

"Dr. Cooper is waiting to talk to you," she responded and then motioned for Melanie to go to the triage area.

The curtain was partially pulled back and as soon as she got close, a middle-aged man stepped out to greet her. "Miss Harper? I'm Dr. Cooper." He shook her hand.

Melanie tried to look around him and into the area to see Josiah, but Dr. Cooper stepped farther out into the hallway and guided her to follow.

"Your fiancé has two gunshot wounds and a mild concussion."

"Where?" she asked shakily. "Where was he

hit?"

"The first went through the pectoralis minor muscle—that's the muscle in the upper arm. It avoided any bones, arteries, and nerves—which is a good thing. It appears to be a clean in-and-out gunshot wound, leaving no shrapnel within the body."

That made her feel mildly better.

"And the other?"

"The other grazed his shoulder," he replied. "He was extremely fortunate."

"Can I see him now?"

With a nod, he stepped aside.

With a murmured thanks, she moved around him and went directly to Josiah's bedside and then openly cried at the sight of him. His eyes were closed and he looked pale. His clothes were covered in blood. She must have whispered his name because his head turned slightly toward her and his eyes fluttered open. Never in her life had she been so thankful to see those brown eyes open.

"Hey," he said softly. He tried to move but immediately winced with pain.

"No, no, no," she said quickly, soothingly. "Don't try to move, okay?" It was hard to stop herself from touching him everywhere just to confirm that he was all right. Her eyes scanned him from head to toe just in case the paramedics and doctors missed anything. When Melanie looked up and met Josiah's gaze, she saw nothing but tenderness there.

"I'm going to be okay, Mel. It was a clean shot."

She nodded, but couldn't seem to make herself speak. She was shaking and overwhelmed and felt completely helpless. Her hands hovered over him—not wanting to touch him directly in case he was in any pain. Thankfully, he took pity on her and slowly reached out and guided her hand down onto his thigh and then covered it with his own.

"It's going to be all right," he said softly. "I promise."

And then she finally felt in control of her emotions enough to speak. "I was so scared, Josiah. I had no idea what happened to you and the drive over felt like it took ten lifetimes!" She explained how her father had been the one to come and get her and bring her to the hospital. "I wish I had gotten here faster."

"I wish you didn't need to be here, sweetheart," he said gruffly. "I hate that you're upset."

Her eyes went wide. "Josiah, my being upset is nothing compared to what you're going through."

He chuckled and then winced. "Um…yeah. Probably should wish that I hadn't been shot, huh?"

"Ya think?" she teased even as tears streamed down her face.

"Unfortunately, I can't turn back time and this is what I have to deal with," he said, his eyes closing slightly. "I'm fortunate this is all that happened. I'll be uncomfortable for a while and my arm will be in a sling, but in a few weeks, I'll be as good as new. Probably just in time for the Christmas parade, but my waving will be at a minimum."

With an exaggerated wink at her, Melanie

couldn't help but laugh at his attempt at humor. "Only you would be concerned about being able to wave in a parade."

"You were the one who once told me you thought I deserved my own fan club..."

"No, what I said was that it was like you have your own fan club around here. That's completely different."

But he ignored her and continued. "You said I should have a parade in my honor."

Now she laughed a little harder. "I think you have more than a mild concussion because you have a seriously warped memory of that conversation."

He shook his head. "Nope, I distinctly remember you saying I should have a parade in my honor."

"Don't even," she said, wiping the last of her tears away. "I believe what I said was maybe there was a parade in your honor during one of those ridiculous Christmas festivals. Then we joked about the marching band following you around and you said only on Saturdays." Then she smiled tenderly at him. "But in light of what happened today, I think you totally deserve a parade in your honor."

"That's my girl," he whispered.

"When can we take you home?" she asked. "Has anyone talked to you about it yet?"

"No, but..."

Behind them, Dr. Cooper came back into the room. "Okay, Mr. Stone, let's see how you're doing."

Melanie stepped out of the way and had to rein

herself in every time she saw Josiah wince with pain when Dr. Cooper touched him. Hadn't he been through enough? Shouldn't they give him something for the pain?

Clearly she'd said all of that out loud because Dr. Cooper turned to her and gave her a patient smile. "Why don't you step out into the hall while we do this?"

Melanie looked beyond him to Josiah who nodded. "You should go and tell your dad what's going on and I think Drew is out there as well. Tell them all that I'm fine and I'm hoping I'll go home later today."

"Tomorrow," Dr. Cooper said as he continued to examine the wound. "We'll keep you overnight for observation and send you home tomorrow with care instructions, antibiotics, and pain meds if you need them."

Josiah grinned weakly at Melanie. "One night. That's not so bad, right?"

She hated it, but she needed to be strong and not let him see her break down.

Again.

"Not bad at all," she said. "I'll come back in a few minutes."

Out in the waiting room, she did exactly as Josiah asked and gave her father and Drew an update. Drew excused himself to call the station while John guided Melanie to a seating area and encouraged her to sit and relax.

"He's very lucky," John said.

Melanie looked at her father like he was crazy. "Dad, he got shot! How is that lucky?"

"It could have been much worse, Mel. It could have…" He stopped and shook his head. "I don't even want to think about it. We need to be thankful that he's going to be okay. One night in the hospital and a couple of weeks' worth of recovery are nothing in the grand scheme of things."

She knew her father was right, but this was all too hard to wrap her brain around. Just this morning they were happy and laughing and planning their wedding and in the blink of an eye, they had almost lost everything.

She almost lost him.

And that's when she started to cry again.

As if knowing exactly what she was feeling, her father wrapped her in his arms and simply held her while she cried.

## Chapter Five

Three days later, Josiah thought he was going to go insane.

He was home and just about everyone in Silver Bell Falls had stopped by to see him. It was a good thing—a great thing!—but he was beginning to get a little stir crazy.

"Dude, you seriously need to relax."

Looking over at his friend Dean Hughes, Josiah frowned. "That's all I've been doing—relaxing. I hate it. I need to be up and doing something. Anything!"

Dean simply laughed softly. "We were all afraid of this."

Josiah simply arched a dark brow at the comment.

"Look, we all know how involved you are in the community and you're a great sheriff. And as much as I hate to say it…we've all been taking bets on how long you were going to stay at home before you started complaining."

"He was complaining three hours after he got shot," Melanie commented as she put a plate of cookies down on the table for the men to share. Then she winked at Josiah. "The nurses at the hospital were glad to see him go."

Dean laughed again. "Really? Our mild-mannered sheriff upset some of the fine citizens of Silver Bell?"

"Let's just say there's been a decrease in his fan club," Melanie teased.

"Ah-ha! So you admit I have a fan club!" Josiah quipped.

But Melanie simply pat his cheek and gave him a serene smile. "Sure. If that will make you feel better, then yes. You have a fan club."

While he knew she was just saying it to make him happy, he'd still count it as a victory—something he didn't have a lot of this week.

"Josiah, you have to give yourself time to heal. I know it sucks and you're anxious to get back to work but…you're not going to be of any use to anyone if you're in pain," Dean said reasonably.

And while he knew his friend was right, it wasn't what he wanted to hear. Actually, everyone who came through their house and visited him in the hospital had all said the same thing, but he couldn't help but feel frustrated. If just one person would agree with him—even if it didn't lead to him going back to work any sooner—he'd still feel better.

"It's my left shoulder," Josiah argued. "I'm right-handed. I can still do almost everything that I need to do. What is the big deal about going down to the station and being in my office and just…supervising?"

"You can't drive," Melanie reminded him. "And Dr. Cooper said you need to give your body time to heal properly. There's still a risk for infection. Can't you just…?" Her words were cut off by the ringing of her cell phone. She excused herself and took the call in the other room.

"Melanie's right," Dean said.

"Then I need something to do," he grumbled. "I can only read and watch TV for so long. Mel's got a book she's working on and I can't monopolize all her time."

"There isn't anything I can do or say that's going to make you feel better," Dean said after a minute. "I get your frustration but you have to trust that the doctors know what they're talking about."

"Yeah. I know." He went to slouch in his seat but it pulled at the wound and he hissed with pain.

Dean leaned forward and snatched up a cookie. "And that should be an immediate reminder of why you need to take it easy."

"Okay, fine. Distract me. How's Abby? How's Maya?"

Relaxing back in his chair, Dean smiled. "They are deep in dance mode for the big Christmas recital. Practice has already begun and there is a lot of pink tulle around my house."

Dean's wife owned a dance studio in town and when he had gotten custody of his niece after his sister died, he had been introduced to Abby and the world of ballet. They had gotten married just after Christmas last year and he'd never seen his friend look so happy.

"Isn't there always?" Josiah teased.

Nodding, Dean reached for another cookie. "Definitely, but whenever there's a recital in the works, it seems to multiply."

"And you love every minute of it."

"Damn right I do."

"So what's next for you guys? You know, after recital season is over."

Dean shrugged. "We're looking to move into a bigger house. We want to stay close to town so Maya won't have to change schools but…it's time to find a place that's ours—that all three of us have a say in." He looked around the room. "I love what you and Melanie built here. It's bright and open and it's kind of what we're thinking of."

"If you're not in a hurry then you should consider building. I swear there were times when it made us crazy, but in the end, the results were worth it."

Another shrug. "Maybe. Although now that we've almost got our first year of marriage under our belts, I think we can take on the task of possibly designing our own place. I'm sure Abby would love to have dance space, Maya wants a playroom of her own, and…" He paused. "And we're going to need a nursery."

It took Josiah a minute to comprehend what Dean was saying but when he did, he couldn't help but smile and reach out a hand to him. "Really?

That's great news! Congratulations!"

With a grin, Dean shook his hand. "Thanks. We're just starting to tell people but Abby's about eight weeks along. She's feeling good and other than worrying about how she'll teach classes when she's further along, we're both really excited. Maya is too."

And that right there was what Josiah wanted more than anything with Melanie, to be married and settled in and starting a family. He wasn't about to add the whole starting a family thing to their plates when they had yet to decide on a wedding date, but it was there in the back of his mind.

"So when is the…"

"Sorry about that," Melanie said as she breezed back into the room. She looked a little frazzled and Josiah's attention was immediately on her.

"Is everything okay?"

Without making eye contact with him, she sat down and fidgeted with her hair. "Uh-huh. Everything's fine." Smiling at Dean, she asked, "How are your girls doing?"

Dean must have sensed that something was up too because he glanced at Josiah before responding. He told her the news about the baby and while Melanie squealed with excitement, Josiah still felt like something was up. Who was on the phone? What was it about? It was obvious that she wasn't going to talk about it while they had company so he had no choice but to bide his time.

Twenty minutes later, with Dean out the door, Josiah immediately pounced. "Now can we talk about what upset you on the phone?"

Frowning, Melanie sat down on the sofa and looked at Josiah. "It was Christine on the phone." It wasn't unusual for her editor to call her, but when she did it was normally to discuss edits or deadlines. She wasn't due for either of those things.

"What did she want? You're on track with this book and you're done with the edits on the last manuscript so...what's going on?"

If this were any other time, she wouldn't hesitate to tell him. But with the shooting and him being so miserable...well...the timing of this call really sucked.

"There's been some interest in the movie rights to my first book," she said carefully. "Actually, we've been in talks with a production company for a couple of months now."

Josiah's eyes went wide. "What? Why haven't you said anything?" Then he smiled. "This is amazing news!"

Melanie could feel herself blush. "I didn't want to get my hopes up. You hear of this sort of thing all the time and more often than not, it doesn't amount to anything."

"But still, Mel, this time it could!"

She nodded. "That's why Christine was calling. We have an offer and they are motivated to start filming in the spring." With a soft sigh, she looked at him helplessly. "She wants me to go to Manhattan and meet with her and the producers to sign contracts."

"That's fantastic!" He stood and walked over to her and gently pulled her to her feet with his good arm. Wrapping it around her, he said, "I'm so proud of you!"

Mindful of his wounds, Melanie gently hugged him back. This was really good news for her—for her career—but she hated the thought of traveling right now and leaving Josiah home alone. On the few trips she'd had to make to meet with Christine, he'd never come with her. It was always easier for her to go alone and he didn't particularly enjoy walking around the crowded city—especially when she was in meetings all day. He was quite possibly the only person who couldn't find something to do in the city that never slept.

Go figure.

Together, they sat down on the sofa. "So when do you need to go?" he asked. "Is there a rush?"

"I think if I said I couldn't go right now, Christine would do what she could to reschedule. But as it stands right now, she's got a meeting scheduled for Monday."

"Okay, wow. That's five days away." He looked at her expectantly. "You're gonna go, right?"

She hesitated ever-so-slightly and Josiah immediately jumped on it.

"You don't have to worry about me and I certainly don't want you missing out on such an important meeting because of me. I'm fine, Mel. Everyone is making more of a big deal out of this than they need to. Even the doctor said he couldn't believe what a clean wound it is—the bullet didn't hit anything vital. I just have to baby my shoulder for a few weeks."

"Josiah, I know that but it doesn't mean I want to just pick up and leave you so soon. Your arm is in a sling and there are a lot of things you still can't do on your own. I mean…you can't drive and you certainly can't cook with just one hand. What if you needed help with something and I wasn't here and…"

"Okay, okay, okay," he said softly, soothingly. "I get it. I do. And as much as I appreciate how you want to take care of me, Mel, you have a job to do and you need to be able to do it. I'm sure your dad could come and stay with me. It won't be a big deal."

"It's a big deal to me," she murmured. Studying him hard, she said, "If I was injured, would you leave?"

Melanie didn't even have to wait for his answer. She saw it in his eyes.

Never.

He would never leave her.

"Don't ask me to," she said firmly. "If I have to, I can Skype the meeting with Christine. I told her what was going on here and she understands. We've handled contract negotiations via email before and we can do it again."

And they had. Granted, they were standard publishing contracts that she'd been signing with her publisher for years and there wasn't anything new other than more money in advances, but Melanie still felt confident they could handle movie negotiations the same way. She would talk to Christine beforehand and talk about what they were offering and if she had any counter offer and see how much creative control she was going to have and…it should all be okay, right? What benefit could there possibly be to her going and meeting with these people in person?

And on top of that, there was so much for Melanie to be handling here at home. Besides taking care of Josiah, she did still have a book to write. If she took time off to go to Manhattan, chances are she'd go a few days before the meeting and stay for a day or two after to take in the city and it was time away from her keyboard that she really couldn't afford to take.

And as if that wasn't enough, they still had a wedding to start planning.

Josiah shifted beside her, his dark eyes studying her.

"What? What are you looking at?"

He gave her a lazy grin. "You looked like you were thinking about something pretty hard there for a minute."

Why deny it? Josiah was scary-good at reading her. "I guess I'm just working it all out in my head—the reasons not to go. We live in a day and age where meetings can be held without everyone involved being in the same room, so really, it makes things so much easier."

"Mel…"

"And Christine is always telling me how I am easily distracted. Like all the time. No doubt if I step away from this book for four or five days, it will take me weeks before I get my groove back. And nobody wants that. Things are going well—the words are flowing and I feel like I'm finally in my characters' heads and it would be crazy of me to think it will all just come back after an extended break."

"Mel..." he repeated with a sigh.

"And we still haven't picked a wedding date!"

That one seemed to shut him up.

Literally.

His mouth snapped shut.

Nodding and smiling with just a hint of victory, she went on. "That's right. We still have to look at the calendar and pick a date. I haven't forgotten that, have you?"

He mutely shook his head.

"And—again—if we don't sit down and do this now like we had planned, it will get pushed aside and then what? Then it will be months or even another year before we talk about it again."

"I don't think that will happen," he argued lightly.

"But you never know! With the distraction of this trip and then the contract and then the book and then the movie...where will it end, Josiah? What happened to you on Sunday should teach us that life is precious. We shouldn't put off tomorrow what we can do today! We need to stop wasting time and take care of the things that matter most!"

She was spiraling; she knew she was spiraling and yet she couldn't stop.

"You are what matters most to me!" she cried, taking his good hand in hers. "Why would I go to

Manhattan and leave you when you need me? Why would I stop being productive at my job when I don't have to?"

This time he did stop her. "Mel, sweetheart, you need to relax a bit. I don't think you've taken a breath in over a minute."

She realized she was a bit breathless…

"But you get what I'm saying, right?" she questioned.

"I do, but…I don't know. I still think you should go. It's been a while since you've taken a trip and for all you know, the time away will help with your creativity."

"My creativity is just fine right now, whereas you are not."

Rolling his eyes, he squeezed her hand. "I love you, Mel, and I love the way you take care of me, but you're worrying for nothing. I'm a grown man and I can take care of myself." Then he shrugged. "You know, if your dad can come and stay though, that would be great."

He had a point, dammit. Her father would come and stay with Josiah in a heartbeat. The two of them would be just fine for a few days and really, she didn't need to take a lot of extra time.

Although…Christmas shopping in Manhattan was kind of awesome.

No! she chided herself. You can go on this trip strictly for business. There was no time for pleasure. Josiah needs you!

With a small sigh, she knew he was right. She'd call her dad and ask him to come and stay for a few days. And he'd agree even though he had a job he had to go to and that would mean Josiah would be on his own most of the day. No doubt he'd try to go down to the station if left to his own devices and...

Wait.

She didn't have to leave him home alone.

He could come to the city with her! They could have a little romantic getaway!

With a happy gasp, she looked at him with a big smile. "Come with me!"

# Chapter Six

Four days later they were walking around Manhattan giddily close to each other as they took in all of the Christmas decorations.

"I can't believe you've never done this before," Melanie said. "With you being such a fan of the holidays and not living all that far away from the city, I would have thought you would have come here at least once in your life."

"I've been to the city before," he mildly corrected, "just never at Christmas. I mean, why? I live in a town that has the greatest celebration. I don't need anything more than that."

She looked up at him as if he were crazy.

And he kind of was.

As much as the little town of Silver Bell Falls was starting to grow on her, there was no way anyone could compare its holiday fanfare to what they were seeing right now. And as much as she wanted to point that out to Josiah, she figured it was one of those things best kept to herself. Instead, Melanie focused on finding them a place to warm up and get something to eat.

"So, what are we in the mood for? You won't find food like this anywhere."

"Now that's something I definitely remember from when I was here last."

"And when was that?"

"I don't know…maybe when I was twelve?"

"Josiah!" she cried. "Seriously, how could that have been the last time you were here? I don't understand that!"

He shrugged his good shoulder. "You know I'm not a touristy kind of guy and coming here, that's what you have to be."

Stopping in her tracks, she turned and faced him. "Then why did you agree to come with me? If you don't enjoy this kind of thing, why bother?"

As Josiah was prone to do, he gave her a patient smile. The man was seriously too laid back and sometimes she wanted to rattle his cage and get more of a response from him.

"I came because I wanted to spend time with you," he said easily. "This is where you needed to be. It's not often that I have a lot of free time and—I'll admit—I was banking up my vacation time and saving it for our honeymoon but…"

"But what? We're still taking a honeymoon," she gently chided him. "And you're on a medical leave of absence right now. No one's counting this against your accumulated time. Because if they are then…"

"Okay, okay, okay," he quickly interrupted and soothed her, gently caressing her cheek. "Don't get all worked up. I wasn't implying that anyone was taking my time away from me."

"Oh," she said with relief. "Okay. Good." Tilting her head a little, she asked, "Then what were you going to say?"

With a soft laugh, Josiah took her hand and started walking again. "I was going to say that we still don't have a wedding date and we haven't talked about honeymoons either." He looked down at her and grinned. "We're seriously bad at this planning thing."

She knew he was right. Even after she used that as part of her argument not to come to the city, once she changed her mind and asked him to come with her, all of their time and energy had been put into making travel plans and making sure Josiah was okay to fly. Then there was a lot of time convincing him how it was okay to be away from town for several days and that crime would not start running rampant if he were gone. His deputies were more than competent and he knew it, but…he didn't want to admit it.

Either way, travel plans had been the hot topic and somehow the wedding talk had gotten postponed.

Again.

"Then it looks like we have a topic for our dinner conversation," she said with a big grin. "So let's…" Her words were cut off when she felt her phone vibrating in her pocket. They stepped to the side of the sidewalk as she pulled it out. "It's Christine," she said, holding up the phone for Josiah to see the screen.

Answering, she listened to her editor while watching Josiah who seemed more than a little unimpressed with the amount of people walking around.

"Uh-huh..."

Why couldn't he just enjoy himself? It wasn't as if she were asking him to move here. This was just a few days of fun, playing tourist and getting away from their everyday life to distract him while he healed.

"So, what do you say?" Christine asked excitedly.

"Um...I'm sorry. What?"

"I said you and Josiah should join me for dinner! There's an amazing Italian restaurant right next to your hotel and I'm not far from there. Come on, Mel. We can all meet up and talk about the meeting tomorrow!"

"Josiah and I are out right now and I'm not sure what our plans are," she said carefully, looking at him to see how he might feel about it.

Reading her mind, he looked at her and nodded. Melanie knew he'd agree to go even if he didn't want to because he was fully supportive of her career, but again, just once she wished he'd be a little unreasonable.

Sighing, she said, "Sure. How about we meet you there in thirty minutes?"

"Perfect! See you then!"

Sliding the phone back into her pocket, she

looked up at him. "You totally could have said no to that."

"You could've too," he countered.

Touché.

"I know," she said wearily, "but she caught me off guard and we were just talking about what we wanted to talk about over dinner and now we can't and…"

"Mel, it's all right. We'll go and have dinner with Christine and then we have all night to talk. Hell, we have the rest of our lives to talk so…we're good."

Frowning, she looked up at him and had a strong urge to stomp her foot. "You know you can get mad at me sometimes, right?"

Now he looked confused. "Why would I be mad at you?"

"Isn't it obvious? It's like I keep finding excuses to keep us from planning our wedding!" Even as the words came out, Melanie was a bit horrified that she was saying them out loud.

The laughter she was met with wasn't quite the response she was expecting either.

"What's so funny?"

"You are," he said, still chuckling.

"I don't see how," she murmured.

"We can both agree that we put off this discussion because we were building the house, right?"

She nodded.

"Then I got shot," he added lightly and Melanie was amazed at how he could even remotely joke about it. "So that sort of put our conversation on hold that day.

"Not funny, Josiah..."

"Then we had to plan the trip," he went on as if she hadn't spoken. "Going to dinner with Christine doesn't mean we can't talk about the wedding. It just means we have to talk about it later."

"Fine. But we have to promise that we will," she urged.

Leaning down, he kissed her soundly and everything in her instantly relaxed as she kissed him back. When he lifted his head, he smiled down at her. "I promise."

And he meant it.

He truly did.

But when Christine was the one to bring up the subject, Josiah couldn't help but smile a bit to himself.

"So?" Christine asked midway through the main course. "Have you guys set the date yet? You're in the new house and all and I know that was what you were waiting for." She looked expectantly between the two of them.

"Funny you should bring it up because that's what we were talking about when you called," Melanie replied around a sip of wine. "This last week has been crazy and it seems like we keep getting distracted."

Nodding, Christine took a sip of her own wine before responding. "Well, I would imagine Josiah's accident took precedence over everything!" Then she looked at Josiah and smiled. "Although I have to admit, if Melanie hadn't told me what happened, gunshot wound would not even cross my mind!"

"I was fortunate," he said, hoping he sounded modest. "It could have been a lot worse." Melanie instantly reached for his hand and he saw the tears in her eyes. They'd spent a lot of time talking about how scared she was and he had to admit, the situation had scared him as well. In all his years of living in Silver Bell Falls and as the sheriff, nothing like this had ever happened. And as much as he tried to comfort Melanie and assure her that he was fine and this was an isolated incident, he knew it was all too new and too fresh in their minds for them to simply gloss over.

Kissing Melanie's hand, he smiled at her and looked at Christine. "It was a clean shot and other than being really sore, I'm good. Now I'll have a couple of weeks off to sit around and hopefully start planning a wedding."

Which—if they ever got to it—would be a great distraction.

Christine's smile was bright as she looked at the two of them. "Do you have any ideas about when you want to do it? A summer wedding? Fall?"

Melanie looked at him briefly before responding. "I was thinking spring—you know, flowers blooming, warmer temperatures…"

"Ooo…that does sound nice." Christine looked at Josiah. "Is that what you're thinking too?"

In that moment, he was almost afraid to look at

Melanie but…

"I was hoping for a Christmas wedding," he said, his gaze focused on Christine and Christine only.

Her eyes went wide and if possible, her smile broadened. "Oh, that would be fantastic! And in your little Christmas town too!" She gasped and then looked at Melanie. "You would make a beautiful winter bride, Melanie!"

Beside him, he heard Melanie's groan but if Christine did, she chose not to comment on it.

"And really, why wait? The two of you have been together for so long now and everyone can see how you were meant to be since the moment you met! On top of that, think of how much of the work would be done for you because everything around you would be so beautifully decorated and…"

Josiah tuned out at that point because he could tell Melanie was only half-listening. He squeezed her hand in encouragement and offered her a smile when she looked at him. Unfortunately, he could tell she was getting a little annoyed at yet another positive response to the mention of a Christmas wedding.

Clearing his throat, he interrupted Christine. "We have a lot to take into consideration, but we hope to make a decision soon." Then he changed the subject to the food they were eating and that seemed to do the trick. The remainder of the meal was spent talking about their meeting tomorrow and all the ways this movie deal would help boost Melanie's career. And at that point, he was more than happy to sit back and listen because really, what he wanted most was for Melanie to be happy and successful.

Writing was a passion of hers and he knew that even though it sometimes came across as being a burden, she loved it. The publishing world was forever changing and it was getting harder for her to find ways to stand out in a sea of talented writers. He hoped this movie would help her achieve her goal.

He was learning so much about her job and he had to admit he had no idea so much went into it. At first glance, he thought, okay, you get an idea for a story and you write it. Boy, was he wrong. There was so much more to it and he was in awe of how talented she was and how she balanced everything she needed to do—writing, editing, marketing, promoting, cover designing…it was exhausting just thinking about it.

When the meal was over, they thanked Christine and promised to see her tomorrow. Well, Melanie did. There was no reason for Josiah to go with her. It wouldn't look particularly professional for him to be there and besides, he planned on doing a little sight-seeing or shopping while she was out. It wasn't his favorite way to pass the time but he figured it was the best option for him.

Since the restaurant was right next to the hotel, their walk back should have been short. All he wanted was to go to their room and relax, but they weren't far from Rockefeller Center and Melanie begged to go see the tree with its lights on.

How could he say no?

The temperature was cold but he was used to

*A Very Married Christmas*

that. The constant throngs of people—however—were really starting to grate on his nerves. But when they turned that corner and the massive Christmas tree came into view, it almost made the whole trip worth it.

Beside him, Melanie chatted excitedly about how beautiful it all was and how she couldn't believe how she'd never noticed it before and he had to admit, he loved hearing that. There was no way he could imagine her going through the rest of her life hating Christmas the way she had when he first met her. And as much as he loved the holiday, it was incredible to be experiencing it through her eyes.

They were overlooking the ice skaters and Josiah stood behind her and wrapped his good arm around her. "It's kind of amazing, isn't it?"

She nodded. "You see it on TV but it doesn't do it justice. I mean…the energy, the vibe in the air is just…it's infectious!"

Chuckling, he placed a kiss on her temple. "I was looking forward to going back to the room, but I'm glad we came down here to see this."

The amount of people walking around them was staggering. Hell, the number of people doing the exact same thing as they were doing—simply standing and watching the skaters—was staggering.

"Look at that couple," she said softly.

He laughed again. "You'll have to be a little more specific. There's a lot of them down there."

"The older couple in the middle. She's wearing a red coat with a white scarf and he's got on the black coat…"

"With the red scarf," he finished for her. They were an elderly couple—although from this distance he'd be hard-pressed to say how old. "I see them."

"Look how happy they are," she said with wonder. "I bet they've been coming here to skate for years."

"It's possible." Although they could be tourists…

"I bet they've been coming here since they were young. Maybe this is where they met and fell in love."

Ah…the romance writer in her was coming out. He wasn't often privy to her creative process and this small glimpse seemed a little like a gift. "You think so, huh?"

Nodding, she said, "I bet right now they're talking about how crowded it is now and how it never used to be this way. He'll complain about it because that's what men do…"

"Hey!"

"And she'll tell him that this is the way it's supposed to be—especially at this time of year." She sighed dreamily. "They'll talk about bringing the grandkids with them next weekend because that's what they do and it will make for a wonderful memory."

If anything, he fell a little more in love with her in that moment. The whimsical side of her was in slight contrast to the practical woman she normally was. He kissed her temple again. "That would definitely make for a wonderful memory."

She nodded again and slowly turned in his arms. "We should have a memory like that."

He looked at her curiously. "I'm not graceful enough on skates under normal conditions. I have a feeling with this sling I'd be at a real disadvantage."

Laughing, she rested her head on his chest. "Not skating," she said softly and when she looked up at him again, all traces of humor were gone and she looked…contemplative. Serious.

"Mel? You okay?"

A slow smile played at her lips. "You know what? I am. I really think I am."

That seemed a little…cryptic, but he decided to wait her out.

"Skating wasn't the memory I was talking about," she said slowly, as if she wanted him to fully understand what she was getting at.

"O-kay…"

"Josiah Stone, you've opened my eyes to a world I had shut off. And as we've walked around the city today all I could think of was how wonderful everything looked, felt." She paused and took a steadying breath and let it out slowly. "And I think…I think we can make something this magical for ourselves."

He was afraid to get his hopes up, afraid he was reading her wrong. "So you're saying…?"

"I'm saying…let's get married for Christmas!"

# Chapter Seven

They were back in Silver Bell Falls and Melanie was a little surprised at how fast news of their plans had traveled.

"Why…does it look like Christmas threw up in here?" she asked cautiously when they walked through their front door.

Beside her, Josiah laughed softly. "I can't say with any great certainty, but if I had to venture a guess, I'd say we have some wedding elves at work."

"Already? We just called my dad to tell him the news. No one else knows!"

Closing the door behind them, Josiah moved into the space. "We called my family too, Mel. They may not live here anymore, but they still have a lot of friends they keep in touch with."

"I suppose," she murmured, looking around at

the two decorated trees, the assortment of Poinsettias, the platters of food, and the fire burning in the ornately-decorated fireplace. "There's music playing, right? I'm not imagining it?"

"There you two are!" John said as he walked out of the laundry room and came over to embrace them. "How was your flight?"

Melanie hugged him distractedly. "It was fine, Dad. What's going on here?"

He grinned sheepishly. "I guess I should have checked with you first…"

"Dad…"

He sighed even as he seemed to look at Josiah for backup. "Fine. I called Lisa and told her you'd made your decision and I booked the barn."

"Oh," she quickly said but then motioned to the room. "This was more of what I was referring to, Dad."

Looking over his shoulder, John let out a nervous chuckle. "This? Um…well, I might have been at the diner when I called Lisa and there were a lot of people around and I guess…" He sighed. "Everyone just started talking at once and volunteering to help the two of you plan the wedding. Things have been arriving all day and I didn't want to hurt anyone's feelings and…"

"John," Josiah said, placing a hand on his future father-in-law's shoulder, "it's okay. This is just the sort of thing that happens in Silver Bell. We're used to it."

"Are we?" Melanie quipped as she began walking around the room. There was something wedding or holiday-related on almost every surface—cookies, candles, candy. It would be rude not to sample them, right? Both her father and Josiah joined her in sampling. "I guess I don't understand why some of this stuff is here."

Josiah raised his hand as he finished chewing. "Planning a wedding can literally take a village. And considering we're doing this on a short timeline, I'm guessing everyone just wants to help."

"Exactly," John said. "Lisa said she can make any changes to the decor in the barn that you want. Hank mentioned—if you're interested—that he can make ornaments for you to give as wedding favors."

"Wow," she said, feeling a little excited at the thought. Hank's ornaments would always hold a special place for her and Josiah, so it seemed only fitting. When she looked at Josiah, she saw he was thinking the same thing. "I think that's perfect."

"Then Dan offered to help with the food if you wanted," John explained.

"I don't know if I want diner food for our wedding," Melanie said with a laugh.

"Oh, come on," Josiah teased. "You know you love the meatloaf."

They all laughed.

"Lisa did mention how she's been working with a lot of locals for events at the barn so I guess some of this stuff is from them," Josiah went on. He snagged another cookie and grinned, "We have to have these at the wedding."

"What about the trees?" she asked her father.

"Bill from the tree lot on Main sent them over. He thought you might like to have some extras this year to use in photos," John said and then motioned to the plants. "He sent those too."

Her head was spinning. While everything here was meant to help her, it just seemed like too much too soon. She wandered around the room and saw samples of invitations and flower arrangements and realized that maybe they had bitten off more than they could chew—which is what she said.

"Melanie," Josiah said softly as he came over and wrapped his arm around her, "that's what makes this whole scene in front of us mean so much more. We're not doing this alone. We have the love, help and support of our entire town to help us. I think we can look around this room and have almost everything planned by tomorrow."

She pulled back. "Are you insane? That's not even possible!"

But Josiah wasn't deterred. "We have the venue and the decorations already done. And as much as I don't think we need invitations, there are enough samples of them right there on the table where we can easily pick one. We're not snobs and we're not complicated people, Mel," he continued. "We're not looking to have some grand, Hollywood-style wedding, right?"

"Right."

"And I'm not saying we have to have it all decided by tomorrow. I'm just suggesting that a lot of the ground work has kind of been done for us."

"I get that and even if we're not having a…what did you just call it…a Hollywood-style wedding, all of this isn't free! We have to pay for all of this stuff."

John cleared his throat. "Can I just say

something here?"

"Of course," Josiah replied.

Looking at his daughter with nothing but sincere affection, he said, "Melanie, you may not believe this, but I have been planning for this day almost since you were born. Even when we were at our poorest, I still put money aside."

She gasped softly.

"It's true," he said with a nod. "Some weeks it was only ten dollars, but I did it."

"Dad...I don't even know what to say." Her heart was beating like mad in her chest at what her father was saying. They had never discussed this sort of thing—weddings or her getting married—and to know that he'd been secretly putting money aside for it was a bit of a shock.

"The money is there for the two of you. It would mean the world to me if you would take it and make this wedding exactly what you want it to be," John said. Melanie was instantly there hugging him.

"I love you, Dad."

"I love you more, kiddo. And I want you to be happy and not have to worry about anything with this wedding."

When they broke apart, Josiah stepped in and hugged him. "I can't thank you enough for this, John. I had money put aside as well, but this just means we can have everything we want for our wedding."

"Or," Melanie interrupted with a grin, "we can plan an amazing honeymoon."

"On that note," John said as he grabbed a

handful of cookies, "I'm going to go and leave the two of you to talk about this."

To say he was overwhelmed would be an understatement.

As soon as John had left, Josiah looked around the living room in awe. His friends had done this for him. For them. The reality of it was more emotional than he would have thought.

Melanie eyed him cautiously. "You okay?"

He shook his head. "I think I'm just…it's all really…" Pausing, he shook his head and looked at her helplessly. "Between the shooting, our trip, and now this? It's a lot to take in."

And she smiled at him—her beautiful blue eyes going soft and a little teary as she looked at him. "I feel that way too. But you know what helps me get through it all?"

Josiah shook his head.

"You." Stepping close to him, Melanie reached up and cupped his cheek in her hand. "The day I met you I was a mess. The news of my grandmother's death, inheriting the cabin, the drive, and just dealing with all the emotions that went with it had me freaking out." She paused. "Then you stormed into my bathroom and threatened to arrest me."

Unable to help himself, he laughed.

"And once we got that misunderstanding cleared up, you became someone I knew I could depend on, rely on. You became my rock. I've leaned on you almost since the beginning, Josiah, and I know there isn't anything I can't handle with you beside me—good or bad." She motioned to all the things around them. "And this is definitely good."

"You think so?"

She nodded. "Personally, I think you talk about the wonders of this town and what they do for others, but this is the first time you're experiencing it for yourself."

"I guess that's possible…"

"Trust me," she said softly, gazing up at him lovingly. "If I had to learn to accept the fact that the people of this town are genuinely good, sincere, and have an abnormal attachment to everything Christmas-related, then you have to too."

There was his sassy girl—she accepted all of those things, but she still thought it odd. He laughed and pulled her in close—cursing how he still had his left arm in a sling. With a kiss on the top of her head, he sighed. "You know it's going to get crazy now, right?"

She nodded. "I do."

Unable to help himself, he smiled. "I like hearing those words."

"You do, huh?" she said silkily. Pulling back, she looked up at him.

"I do."

Her smile was the most beautiful thing in the world to him. "That's good because I like hearing those words come from you too."

"We've always been in sync," he murmured.

With a look around the room, he realized he didn't want to talk about the wedding right now. What he wanted was to celebrate in the sexiest of ways with the woman in his arms. And as Melanie's arms wrapped themselves tighter around him, those words proved right.

Looking down at her he said, "You know, our weekend getaway wasn't nearly as romantic as I would have liked."

"Josiah, you're injured and need to heal. I think it was a wonderful trip just the way it was."

But he shook his head and took a step back. "That was the first time we've gone away together and it was partially spent on business and the rest playing tourist."

The smirk she gave him told him she knew what he was referring to.

"We had a decent hotel room and all we did was sleep in it."

This time she laughed softly. "That's really what they're for."

Then he took one of her hands in his and slowly began to lead her to their bedroom. "True. And it may have been a long time since I spent a night in one, but that doesn't mean I don't know that they can be used for much more than a good night's sleep."

Slowly, she licked her lips and gave him a sassy look. "So you're saying we should have put that room to better use."

Nodding as they made their way through the bedroom door, he said, "Exactly."

But as he pulled her toward the bed, Josiah saw

her hesitation and instantly stopped. The sigh of frustration couldn't be helped.

"You have a follow-up appointment with your doctor tomorrow," she said, concern lacing her tone. "I don't want to do anything that will hinder your healing, Josiah."

"We'll be careful," he said earnestly, slowly pulling the sling off. "I promise."

Melanie did not look convinced.

"You know you're going to be mad at yourself if anything keeps you from going back to work, right?" When she looked at him, he gave no indication that he agreed with her. With an eye roll that was more comical than anything, she looked at him. "I refuse to be held responsible for any setbacks you have."

Carefully, he pulled his shirt over his head. It took a bit of an effort not to grimace. The wounds were healing but having a bullet go right through you meant there were two spots trying to heal and movement of any kind wasn't particularly comfortable. They were both covered in bandages but he knew they were healing fine.

"I'll tell you what," he said, sitting down on the bed. "If it makes you feel any better, I'll let you do all the work."

Her laughter was music to his ears. Taking a step toward him, Josiah thought he almost had her convinced.

"I'm serious," he went on. "I promise to lie back and rest my shoulder and be a good boy."

The sexy grin told him he'd won.

"Well…as long as you behave," she said softly,

kicking her shoes off.

The eager nod he gave her might have felt a little like begging, but he didn't care. It had been a week since they'd last made love and he missed it—missed the intimacy and just being able to touch her and love her like he wanted to.

Moving closer, Melanie peeled her shirt off and shimmied out of her jeans and Josiah actually felt himself break out in a sweat. How was it possible that after all their time together she still had the ability to turn him inside out like this?

A gentle shove on his good shoulder had him slowly lying down on the bed. Straddling him, Melanie leaned down and kissed him and it was slow and wet and a little bit dirty and it was like hitting the launch button. More than anything he wanted to reverse their positions and do all the things to her that he knew drove her wild. It was impossible, but still…a man could dream.

With no warning, she broke the kiss, straightened, and unhooked the lacy bra she was wearing. She tossed it over her shoulder, and the look on her face made every kind of sexy promise that he could imagine.

All thoughts of changing positions left his mind.

"Brace yourself, Sheriff," she said huskily.

Yeah, there was no need to wish for anything else.

Because this was his dream come true.

# Chapter Eight

Looking back, Melanie would say she was glad they took that afternoon and the rest of that day for themselves because the following day began what could only be described as wedding planning on steroids. All it had taken was one phone call to Lisa to confirm the barn and from that point on, Melanie couldn't remember the last time she got to have a conversation that wasn't about the big day.

Now, ten days later and standing in the middle of a bridal boutique back in New York City, she sighed with impatience. She was getting zipped into her tenth gown and was no longer having fun.

"C'mon, Mel," Josiah's sister Danielle said with a grin. "Don't get your tinsel in a tangle. You don't want to make a snap decision on a wedding gown. Most brides take months to do this sort of thing. You knew it was going to be a marathon weekend."

Between the hopping in and out of gowns and the bad holiday puns her future sister-in-law was so proud of, Melanie was certain she'd go out of her mind. At this point, she'd be willing to close her eyes and point at a gown and take it if it meant getting out of this hell.

"I did, but I still had hopes I'd luck out and find something fast," Melanie reasoned as she looked in the mirror and frowned.

Nope. Not her gown.

"I think it's…" Danielle began but Melanie instantly cut her off.

"This isn't it."

"It's not so bad," Danielle reasoned. "I mean, it has some redeeming qualities."

"Like what?" Melanie asked, almost cringing at the amount of lace that was practically choking her.

"It's white."

Melanie couldn't help but laugh. "Good one."

Before she knew it, she was back in the dressing room and stepping out of dress number ten. Hannah, her sales clerk, promised to be right back and with nothing to do other than stand in her underwear, Melanie wondered if she should just give up and get a regular dress—something a little less bridal and a lot more…ready to wear.

That thought lasted a nanosecond because no matter how much she tried to pull off the I'm-not-a-girly-girl thing, she secretly kind of was. And the idea of not wearing a big white gown on her wedding day just wasn't going to work.

"Okay, Miss Harper," Hannah said as she

breezed back in. "This one wasn't part of your original choices, but your future sister-in-law just found it and asked me to show it to you."

Melanie was about to decline when she heard Danielle on the other side of the door.

"Just try it!" she called out. "I'm telling you, it's the one! Trust me! Have I steered you wrong yet?"

It was on the tip of her tongue to remind her how she hadn't really steered her anywhere but kept it to herself. Glancing at the gown, Melanie wasn't sure she was on board. For starters, it was strapless.

"This is more of a summer gown, isn't it?" she quietly asked Hannah.

But not quietly enough. "They have beautiful wraps out here, Mel!" Danielle called out. "And everywhere you go will be heated!"

"Wasn't asking you!" she called back but couldn't hide her amusement with the situation.

"Don't be such an angry elf! Just try it on!"

With a shrug, she looked at Hannah and said, "I guess I'm trying it on."

It took all of two minutes when she knew.

This was her gown.

With a soft gasp, Melanie studied her reflection and looked over at Hannah who nodded approvingly.

"I heard that!" Danielle yelled. "I heard you gasp! I was right, wasn't I? It's the one!"

"Let her in," Melanie murmured, unwilling to take her eyes off of the mirror. She turned and studied the gown from every angle. It had a satin bodice, chapel train, and lavish organza ball gown skirt with beautiful beaded and embroidered details.

"It looks even better than I imagined," Danielle said with a hint of awe as she walked around Melanie. "I'm telling you, with your hair up and one of those winter wraps, you're going to look stunning."

In that moment, Melanie believed her.

"You aren't going to need a lot of alterations," Hannah said. "Other than the length, the bodice fits you perfectly."

"Can you grab a couple of wraps for her to try on?" Danielle asked and once Hannah left the room, she gave Melanie a knowing smile. "See, ye of little faith? We found it! Well…technically, I found it. Just promise to name your firstborn after me and we'll call it even."

Laughing, Melanie said, "One thing at a time, Dani, please. Let me get through this wedding and then we can talk about babies, okay?"

Danielle let out a happy little squeal and danced in place. "This is just so exciting!! My brother's getting married at Christmas! It's like the greatest thing ever!"

"So weird," Melanie mumbled.

"You're doing it again."

"Doing what?"

"Being an angry elf," Danielle deadpanned. "So stop it. You're not allowed to pout when you're in a wedding gown."

"Somehow I don't think that's a rule…"

"You know…you better not pout, you better not cry, you better not…"

"That's a Christmas song," Melanie said

wearily. "And it has nothing to do with weddings."

"Rules still apply." With a smug look of satisfaction, she took a step back as Hannah came back with several options for wintery wraps. "And when we're done here, we are going to go and have a glass of wine to celebrate!"

"As long as it comes with room service so I can be in my yoga pants, a t-shirt, and no bra, I'm in!"

Josiah was in his own kind of hell that had nothing to do with wedding planning.

He was at his third doctor appointment since the shooting and his doctor refused to sign off on letting him go back to work. It didn't matter how much he explained how he was strictly going to be doing desk work and wouldn't be doing any kind of patrolling or active duty. As he sat on the exam table, he did his best not to let his frustration show.

"Doc, I'm hardly wearing the sling and you said yourself how my arm is healing nicely. We're in full holiday swing here in town and my guys need me. They're all working overtime to coordinate the parade and all the festivities. I don't see what the harm is in sitting at my desk."

To his credit, Dr. Bailey—his longtime physician—barely reacted to his speech. "Josiah, I'm doing this for your own good. Melanie would kill me if I let you go back to work and something happened before your wedding."

"Melanie knows how much I want to go back

*A Very Married Christmas*

to work." He sighed. "The wedding is two weeks away. And we all know the most activity we have around here is directing traffic. I promise not to leave my desk."

But Dr. Bailey wasn't listening; he was making notes in Josiah's chart. "I'm sorry, Josiah, but I think it's best if you wait until after you come back from your honeymoon and simply start fresh in the new year." He closed the chart and smiled. "Personally, I wouldn't want to do anything to upset the bride—especially since she's been stressed out enough with this last-minute wedding."

For a moment, Josiah studied him. It wasn't that he was saying anything odd but…it kind of was. For starters, while it was pretty much public knowledge around town that he and Melanie were getting married, Dr. Bailey had never taken such an interest in his personal life before. And while he had met Melanie several times, he seemed to be awfully concerned with her feelings right now.

Something was off here but for the life of him, Josiah couldn't put his finger on what it was.

"I really wish you'd reconsider," he said finally, as he stood and put his shirt back on.

With a patient smile, Dr. Bailey collected his things and made his way to the exam room door. "Trust me on this one, Josiah. It will be better for everyone for you to rest a bit longer."

Once Josiah was alone in the room, he wanted to howl with frustration. How could his being miserable be better for everyone? His town needed him! His deputies needed him! But more than that, he needed to get back to business as usual before he lost his damn mind! This was too much down time and it would be one thing if he were seriously injured, but he wasn't. There was some tightness as the wounds healed but that was normal. He had almost complete range of motion and he felt fine. Why was Dr. Bailey being so damn cautious?

The whole way home he grumbled and his mind raced with how he was going to get around the restrictions and get back to work. Distractedly, he waved to the people he passed and by the time he turned off the main road and his house came into view, he felt mildly better. He knew he could walk through the door and commiserate with Melanie and she'd make him feel better. She always did.

John's car was in the driveway but that wasn't anything new. He had been amazing with all of his help with the wedding plans and keeping Melanie from freaking out too much. As he pulled up and then climbed from his truck, he racked his brain on why John might be here today. Were they supposed to go over anything specific for the wedding that he'd forgotten about?

"Hey!" Melanie said as she walked over to kiss him. "How'd the appointment go?"

Closing the door behind him, Josiah frowned.

"That good, huh?" she asked, stepping aside and then following him into the living room where he greeted John.

Taking a seat on the sofa, he rested his head against the cushions and sighed. "I still can't go back to work."

John sat down beside him and frowned. "Why not? You said you were feeling better and everything was looking good."

"That's what I thought," Josiah said wearily. "But all Dr. Bailey would talk about is how I should wait until after the new year and not add any more stress to all the wedding plans." He looked directly at Melanie. "Apparently he thinks my going back to work will freak you out."

And then he noticed the nervous look between Melanie and her dad.

Slowly, he straightened. "Why would he think that?" First he looked at Melanie and then John. And that's when it hit him—John was good friends with Dr. Bailey. They played poker together on Friday nights. Dammit!

"Josiah, there's no harm in taking it easy for a little longer," Melanie began cautiously. "We have so much to do and I don't think we could have accomplished so much if you weren't here to help me."

"Did you ask Dr. Bailey to stall my return to work?" he asked her, point blank.

"Josiah..."

"Did you?" he demanded, coming to his feet.

"It wasn't like that," she said defensively and was about to say more, but John jumped up and came to her defense.

"This isn't necessarily a bad thing, Josiah," John began. "Think about it. When you return to work after the new year, you can be completely focused on your job. Right now, there are too many things that are a distraction. Isn't it better to just wait? What's a few more weeks?"

As much as he wanted to hear what else

Melanie had to say, he turned to John. "There's no reason for me to be sitting around, John! I have a job to do! One that I take seriously and instead of letting me get back to it like I need to, apparently I have people second-guessing me and going behind my back! And it's not for my own good, but for theirs!" His voice rose with every word he spoke and both father and daughter winced at his tone.

"Now wait a minute," John said but Melanie cut him off.

"Dad? I think you should go. Josiah and I need to talk," she said, her eyes never leaving Josiah's.

"I don't think…"

"It's okay," she said. "Really. This is between the two of us."

At first, Josiah didn't think John would go, but ultimately he did. But he gave Josiah a warning glare as he made his way to the door.

Neither spoke for a solid minute after the door closed, but soon Josiah couldn't take the silence any longer. "What the hell were you thinking?" he yelled. "You know how much my job means to me! And I have never—not once—ever interfered with your work! How could you do this to me?"

"I'm just looking out for you!" she argued. "I know you're anxious to go back to work and I'm just not sure you're being honest with yourself about how good you feel! I think you could very well be telling yourself you're fine even if you're not just to get back down to the station!"

"Why would I do that to myself? Believe me, I wouldn't try to go back to work if I wasn't ready for it, Mel!"

She let out a huff of frustration. "Yes, you would! You were trying to go back to work three days after you got shot! Shot!" she cried for emphasis.

"Okay, fine. That wasn't the smartest thing for me to do, but in my defense, I still believe I can sit at my desk just as safely as I can sit here on my own couch!"

Pacing, Melanie looked ready to pull her hair out. "Yes, but here on your own couch you won't be tempted to run out if there's a robbery in progress or…or…someone speeds through town or…or…or to chase down a suspected murderer!" Her voice was trembling and when she looked at him, tears were streaming down her face and that's when he realized what this was all about.

She was scared.

And as much as he wanted to be angry—wanted to argue his case—he couldn't.

He whispered her name as he walked over and wrapped her in his arms. Weeping openly, Melanie shook her head against his chest.

"I was so scared," she sobbed. "Never in my life have I ever been so scared. Please don't make me go through that again. Please."

All he could do was hold her close and wonder how they were supposed to move on from this.

# Chapter Nine

With three days to go until the wedding, things still hadn't righted themselves.

To the casual observer, everyone was happy, everyone was in love and everyone was counting down the days until the wedding. They'd gone to the annual Christmas parade and walked around hand in hand and talked to just about everyone in town. Afterwards, they strolled around the craft fair and bought a ton of stuff to support some of their favorite vendors.

Only Melanie and Josiah knew that right now it was simply a distraction for the emotional storm Josiah's accident had unleashed. She had cried until she didn't have any tears left and through it all, Josiah had held her. But at the end of the day, she knew he was going to have to go back to work eventually. Her talking to Dr. Bailey had only been a temporary fix.

It was one week until the wedding. Looking around the house, she still couldn't believe it. Not only were they decorated for Christmas, but all around them were wedding gifts friends and family who couldn't make the wedding had sent to them. Outside, snow was falling and everything was peaceful.

In a matter of days, they would be married and the day after Christmas they were leaving for their honeymoon. It had long since been a desire for the both of them to go someplace tropical, but with the short notice and the holidays, it had been hard to find the perfect place to go. So they were going to Key West for a week. It wasn't Hawaii, but at least it was going to be warm.

Josiah cleared his throat as he walked into the kitchen where Melanie was looking out at the falling snow. She didn't turn to look at him, but as he moved in close behind her and wrapped his arms around her, two things hit her at once. First, he smelled really good. He always did right after he came out of the shower and it was one of the things she loved about him.

The second was that he had his badge on.

She instantly stiffened in his arms.

"I'm going down to the station," he said carefully, his voice low and a little gruff. "Jared's mom slipped and fell on the ice this morning and he has no one to cover for him. So I'm going in."

Everything in her wanted to rail and scream and beg him not to go.

Three days.

They had only three days until their wedding and all she wanted was for him to be safe.

Instead of making a scene, Melanie swallowed the lump of emotion in her throat and simply nodded.

Kissing the top of her head, Josiah said, "I'll be home for dinner."

She didn't move until the front door closed behind him.

And even then it was only to reach for the chair behind her and slowly sit.

He must have planned his departure just right because before Melanie could even begin to agonize over his leaving, the doorbell rang.

And then it became utter chaos.

The first to arrive was Erika Jacobs—she owned the local bookstore and had become a very good friend. She walked in carrying a large box.

"Brace yourself, buttercup, I need you to sign about two dozen books," she said, placing the box on Melanie's coffee table.

"Um…what?"

Erika motioned to the box. "I'm donating books to a fundraiser in Albany and I promised them signed books. In all the holiday madness, I had forgotten about it. So…here I am!" Her smile was bright and infectious and it was exactly what Melanie needed.

She was about to sit down and start signing when the bell rang again.

This time it was Abby—Dean's wife—along with Kathy from the dance studio.

"I know we should have called first," Abby

said as they walked in the door, "but it occurred to me that with all the last-minute wedding planning, we didn't have time to throw you a shower or even a bachelorette party!"

While Melanie had thought about those things—briefly—they weren't overly important to her—which is what she was about to say when she noticed about a dozen cars pulling up to the house.

"So we're doing that now!" both Abby and Kathy said together.

"Um…what?" Melanie croaked, thankful she had showered earlier and wasn't still in her pajamas.

"It's true!" Kathy said excitedly. "We rounded up as many people as we could for an impromptu bachelorette shower!"

"Is that a thing?" Melanie asked nervously, even as she began greeting her guests.

If it wasn't before, it certainly was now. In the blink of an eye, her entire living room and kitchen were filled up with so many familiar faces. All of these amazing people had given up part of their day to come be with her.

Melanie wasn't stupid—she knew Josiah had to have done this. The timing was just too convenient. And yet in that moment, she knew he did it because he loved her and wanted her to be okay.

"Is every place in town closed today?" she asked after a minute, but her heart felt so full that she couldn't believe this was happening. Bev and Ramona were here from the diner and carried in several trays of food. Donna and Rhonda from the ice cream place followed with what looked like a ton of frozen treats.

"We rearranged some classes today," Abby said from beside her, "so Eileen, Kim, and Shannon could be here too." She wrapped an arm around Melanie and smiled. "It may not be the most organized party, but I can tell you're surprised!"

"More than you know!"

Monique and Jennifer from the antique store were setting up paper goods, Carolyn and Shawn—whose husbands owned the hardware store in town—were quickly hanging decorations. Lynn, Patty, Amanda, and Ciara who all owned the local cleaning business were moving things around to make room for more chairs. Her entire home was being turned upside down and she was too excited to care!

"Hey, Melanie!" Pam from the copy place said as she walked over. "I dropped off the place cards we printed for you over at Lisa's on my way over."

"Thank you!"

"And don't forget your mani-pedi for tomorrow," Shari said as she made her way by. "We've got the salon stocked with champagne and chocolates just for you!"

"Oh, my! That sounds wonderful!"

Dana—who owned the salon along with Shari and Kristy—added, "It will be! I wasn't even supposed to work tomorrow, but I'll be there!"

It didn't look like anyone else could possibly fit, but the door opened and her friend Laura walked in carrying a large box.

"Don't panic, everyone, I have cake!" Laura called out, and the room erupted in cheers of delight.

Abby ushered Melanie into the living room and into one of the oversized chairs that had been designated as the place of honor. Conversation flowed all around as people marveled at the house, the décor, and how she and Josiah had managed to plan a wedding in less than two months.

"It wasn't easy," Melanie said and the entire room seemed to quiet down. She looked out at all the smiling faces and felt tears stinging her eyes. "We couldn't have done it without all of you. I still can't believe how much you all have done."

"That's what friends are for," Dawn from the post office said.

"Here, here!" Gwen, Tina, Lindsay, and Joni cheered. They all worked at the gym in town and Melanie had gone to many spin classes with them.

When she remembered to go.

There was conversation in the kitchen from the ladies who were setting up the food and Melanie turned to Abby and said, "I hate that they're in there working. Can't we ask them to stop and relax for a bit?"

Bev overheard and laughed softly. "Are you kidding? They are setting up as quick as possible because Dan sent over some of his best food. And it's fresh!"

Everyone laughed.

"Please tell Molly, Marybeth, and Denise not to make themselves crazy," Melanie said. "I'm sure everything's going to be wonderful."

"Oh, it will be," her good friend Heather said from beside her. "Besides the food Dan sent, Kay,

Priya, and Amy brought their homemade cookies. Janeen made some of her famous hot apple cider and Isha, Alima, and Cindy brought the wine!"

"Oh my goodness," Melanie said, laughing. "It sounds like we have everything covered!"

"We thought about getting you a male stripper," Anita from the bank called out, "but Debbie said you wouldn't need that since you're marrying the sexy sheriff!"

Even as she laughed, Melanie could feel her cheeks heat. Yes, she was indeed marrying the sexy sheriff and when he got home later, she was going to show just how sexy she thought he was and how much she appreciated all that he did for her today.

Being back at the station felt great.

Sitting behind his desk felt great.

Talking to his deputies and getting things done felt great.

And yet all he could think about was Melanie. No doubt by now she was surrounded by most of the female population of Silver Bell Falls and having a great time, but he kind of felt guilty for ambushing her like that. He'd like to say he had done it for completely selfless reasons, but he'd be lying. It just so happened that he was able to make it all come together so he could return to work—after a much-heated debate with Dr. Bailey—without feeling any guilt.

Boy had that backfired.

He was riddled with it right now.

As the day wore on, he kept busy. But when Drew came in to relieve him, Josiah found he was more than anxious to leave.

"See you at the wedding!" Drew called out and Josiah thanked him on his way out the door.

He drove home and wondered if Melanie was going to be happy to see him or if she was going to give him hell for going to work in such a sneaky manner.

He knew his answer as soon as he walked through the door.

"Hey..." she said, drawing out the word. "There's my sexy sheriff!"

With a soft chuckle, Josiah closed the door behind him and leaned against it. The house was tidied up, but you could tell there had been a party here.

She walked slowly toward him and at first he thought she was trying to be sexy, then he realized she may be a little bit tipsy. When she reached him, Melanie placed her hands on his chest and gave him a bit of a sloppy grin. "Did you catch any bad guys today? Use your handcuffs?" Then she giggled. "You should use them on me!"

Doing his best to keep a straight face, he asked, "Any particular reason I should cuff you?"

Her eyes went wide as she attempted to be serious. "I've been a bad girl today. A very...bad...girl."

So many things raced through his mind—sexy things, naughty things—but he wanted to see where she was going with this.

"Oh really?" Slowly, he reached for his handcuffs. "Do tell."

Taking an unsteady step back, Melanie looked up at him. "There was a party," she said in a loud whisper. "And there was a lot of food. And I ate all of it." Then she shook her head. "My gown isn't going to fit." Then she laughed and walked back into the living room. "And I had wine! Only a glass and then I switched to the cider but someone spiked it!"

Great. Tipsy women were driving all over Silver Bell Falls thanks to him.

Now he was going to worry if everyone got home safely.

Melanie kicked off one shoe and then the other—both flying high in different directions. "I got a lot of lingerie as presents," she said. "Want me to model some of them for you?" Then she tripped over several boxes and immediately righted herself and held up a red lacy bra.

He had a feeling she'd hurt herself at this point if he said yes.

"Tell you what," he began and slowly made his way across the room toward her. "How about we have some coffee and sit and relax and you can tell me all about the party. How does that sound?"

"Boring," she pouted. "There's a lot of lace here and you really need to see it."

Josiah guided her to the couch to sit down. "I promise to let you model it all week in Key West, okay? For now, let's focus on getting some coffee in you."

She sat down, but she didn't look happy about

it. Leaving her there, he went into the kitchen and marveled at the amount of food there was on every surface—cakes, cookies, pies, and covered dishes. At least he wouldn't have to cook tonight.

Or tomorrow.

Either way, it was going to take a long time to clean up.

This is what he got for being sneaky.

A few minutes later he walked back into the living room with coffee in hand and found Melanie asleep. He couldn't help but smile. Slowly he walked over and placed the coffee mug down on the table and knelt in front of her. He caressed her cheek and she let out a sleepy hum.

"I hope you had a good day, beautiful girl," he whispered.

"Mmm…"

Then he stood and gently maneuvered her until she was lying down and covered her with the chenille throw they had over the back of the sofa. She snuggled into it and sighed. Part of him wanted to snuggle in with her, but as he straightened and looked around the house, he knew there were more important things to do.

Like try to restore order to the place.

Somehow, keeping the order in Silver Bell Falls seemed much easier

# Chapter Ten

"Are you ready?"

Melanie nodded.

Beside her, John laughed softly. "Are you sure?"

She nodded again.

They stood at the doors to the church and Melanie's heart beat like wild. This was it. This was her wedding day.

Her Christmas wedding day.

Turning to her father, she studied him. He looked so handsome in his tuxedo and in that moment, she realized just how much he had changed in the last two years, how much they both had.

Swallowing hard, she asked, "Did you ever think we'd be here?"

John looked at her curiously. "What do you

mean?"

"I mean...here," she replied.

"On your wedding day? Of course. I told you, I've been thinking of this since you were a little girl."

"Not just the wedding but...here. In Silver Bell Falls. And on Christmas!" Then she laughed quietly and shook her head before looking at him again. "Did you ever think we'd celebrate Christmas again?"

His expression softened as he looked at her. "Mel, you may not believe this but...I missed celebrating Christmas. I know we had good reasons not to and at the time, I thought it was what was best. But these last few years taught me just how wrong I was. Josiah really opened my eyes to all we'd been missing."

And then she smiled. "He's good like that."

"I know this might not be the time but...I'd like to say how I'm really thankful to your grandmother for bringing us here. It doesn't make up for everything..."

But Melanie quickly interrupted. "Yes it does," she said earnestly. "I'm not going to lie and say I've totally forgiven her, but I'm working on it. In the end, she gave me the greatest gift of all—Josiah."

John's eyes welled with tears as he smiled. "In a million years I never would have imagined you being happy in a place like this—the cold weather and the constant Christmas vibe—but I'm so glad I was wrong. And to think it was here that you found love, Mel...it's the greatest thing in the world for me to see. It's all I ever wished for you. Josiah is a good man and I know how much he loves you and how happy he's going to make you."

She nodded and willed herself not to cry and mess up her makeup. "He really is amazing. He puts up with so much from me and…"

"Oh stop," John immediately said, cutting her off. "You're good for each other—made for each other. Neither one puts up with more than the other. Remember that."

Just then, one of their wedding coordinators—Betty Jo—stepped forward with her hand on the church doors. "Okay, Melanie, everyone's waiting!" And with a smile and a wink, she opened the doors.

The doors opened and Josiah's eyes widened.

She was a vision in white.

His everything.

Melanie Harper was finally going to be his wife and he didn't think he could be any happier than he was at this moment.

With her arm linked with her father's while she carried a massive bouquet of ranunculus, roses, and assorted greenery, she looked like the perfect Christmas bride. Her dark hair was piled high on her head with a sparkling tiara holding it all in place. And her smile? Well, it was directed right at him and he saw everything he wanted there.

Forever.

With her.

When she was finally by his side, all Josiah wanted to do was tell the minister to hurry through the vows so he could kiss her and as her blue eyes sparkled with mischief, he knew she felt the same way too.

He would wait.

He'd been waiting two years for this moment—if not his whole life—what were a few more minutes?

"And now, Josiah will speak the vows he wrote especially for Melanie," the minister said.

Josiah cleared his throat and looked at his bride. "I have always been a firm believer that there is someone out there for everyone. But as I got older, I had started to feel like it was the case for everyone except me. I couldn't understand why it was that all of my family and friends had found their perfect someone and I hadn't." He paused and grinned. "Who knew I'd find her soaking in a bubble bath in Carol Harper's tub."

There was a round of soft laughter throughout the church.

Everyone in town had heard the story before, so he wasn't ashamed to be sharing it now.

Except when the minister looked at him with a hint of disapproval.

Clearing his throat again, he went on. "I knew from the moment I met you that you were going to be important to me. I just didn't realize you were going to be my everything. I love you, Melanie, and I know we've been through a lot together already, but our life together has just begun. And I can't wait to see where the journey takes us."

He placed the ring on her finger and saw her hand trembling.

"And now Melanie will speak the vows she wrote especially for Josiah," the minister said.

She took a steadying breath and let it out slowly. "Josiah Stone, you stormed into my life in a way no one ever had before. And as much as I wanted to resent you, you were exactly what I needed. You always seem to know when to push and when to hold back. You know what I need even before I do." With a small pause, she smiled. "You're my soulmate and I am so thankful each and every day that you came into my life and that you didn't give up on me. I love you and I'm so happy to finally be your wife."

She placed the ring on his finger and, unable to wait another moment, Josiah pulled her in close and kissed her. A round of applause filled the church as the minister declared them man and wife.

Yeah, it was the greatest moment of his life.

The reception was truly like a party in a winter wonderland.

Melanie knew they had been to the barn multiple times since booking the wedding, but until she was standing right there in the middle of it, nothing she had seen had done it justice. The music, the sounds of laughter and the smell of pine in the air was the most festive kind of sensory overload.

Josiah spun her in his arms and leaned down to kiss her on the cheek. "How are you doing, Mrs. Stone?"

"Mmm...I am deliriously happy," she replied. "It's magical in here. So much more than I ever dreamed."

He looked around the room and his smile grew. "I know what you mean. Everyone did an amazing job."

They danced together and talked to guests who surrounded them on the dance floor. When they were alone again a few minutes later, she looked up at him. "Thank you."

"For what?"

"For proving to me time and time again how good things—great things!—can happen on Christmas," she said softly. "I never thought I'd get over all the negative, but you managed to change that and I am so thankful for that. For you. I love you so much."

"I love you too."

They danced a little more and then went and mingled with their guests. Everyone they knew was there and the barn was full to capacity. The music continued to play, food was served, and the atmosphere was both joyful and festive. It was everything Josiah had hoped it would be.

As the night was coming to an end and their guests began to leave, he was mildly disappointed that they weren't dashing off for their honeymoon right away. Tonight they would go home to their house and tomorrow they would have Christmas dinner with their families as if it were a usual Christmas Day. Some would say it was anticlimactic after such a whirlwind, but it was worth waiting a couple of extra days to have had this.

It was after midnight when they were finally home.

He helped her peel off the long fur-lined wrap and she looked like a princess walking across the room to turn the tree lights on. With the room lit only by the tree, she turned and smiled at him.

"It was the perfect day," she said. "It was everything I thought it could be and so much more."

Nodding, he went to her and held her close. "Merry Christmas, Mrs. Stone."

She smiled and snuggled in close to him. "Merry Christmas to you, Mr. Stone." After a moment, she tilted her head back and looked at him. "You know, I was thinking about what we talked about earlier."

He chuckled. "You'll have to narrow that down a bit. We've been talking all day."

"About how you managed to change the way I felt about Christmas. I can honestly say that when I think about it now, I don't think about all the bad ones, only the ones I've had with you."

"I'm so glad I could do that for you," he said, placing another kiss on the tip of her nose. "For a while there, in the beginning, I wasn't sure I'd be able to pull it off. Now I'm glad I did."

"Well," she said with an impish grin, "you may regret doing it."

He frowned. "Why?"

"Let's just say you've set the bar pretty high. The first Christmas you made up for twenty years of missed gifts, last year you proposed and this year we got married. I'm thinking next Christmas is going to be tough. After all, how can you possibly top this?"

An idea came to him out of nowhere but he knew it was perfect.

"I think I know how," he said as he began to lead her toward their bedroom.

Giggling, she put up a little protest. "Ooo…this could work. I mean, it's no dream wedding, but I can get on board with this, Sheriff."

He grinned. "That wasn't quite what I was thinking, Mel," he teased. When they were next to the bed, he slowly spun her around so her back was to him and began to unzip her gown. He placed a soft kiss on her shoulder.

"Then what's on your mind?" she asked breathlessly as his mouth began to rain kisses down her spine.

"I was thinking how maybe next year we'll be celebrating Christmas with a new member of the family. A tiny one. One we make together."

She shivered and sighed as he straightened behind her. With a glance over her shoulder, she smiled. "Why, Sheriff Stone, I think that may be the best Christmas of them all."

And Josiah knew without a doubt that he'd do whatever it took to make that happen.

# ABOUT THE AUTHOR

Samantha Chase is a New York Times and USA Today bestseller of contemporary romance. She released her debut novel in 2011 and currently has more than forty titles under her belt! When she's not working on a new story, she spends her time reading romances, playing way too many games of Scrabble or Solitaire on Facebook, wearing a tiara while playing with her sassy pug Maylene…oh, and spending time with her husband of 25 years and their two sons in North Carolina.

Where to Find Me:
Website: www.chasing-romance.com
Facebook: www.facebook.com/SamanthaChaseFanClub
Twitter: https://twitter.com/SamanthaChase3
Amazon: http://amzn.to/2lhrtQa
Sign up for my mailing list and get exclusive content and chances to win members-only prizes! http://bit.ly/1jqdxPR

# Also by Samantha Chase

## The Enchanted Bridal Series:

The Wedding Season
Friday Night Brides
The Bridal Squad

## The Montgomery Brothers Series:

Wait for Me
Trust in Me
Stay with Me
More of Me
Return to You
Meant for You
I'll Be There

## The Shaughnessy Brothers Series:

Made for Us
Love Walks In
Always My Girl
This is Our Song
Sky Full of Stars
Holiday Spice

## Band on the Run Series:

One More Kiss

## The Christmas Cottage Series:

The Christmas Cottage
Ever After

## Silver Bell Falls Series:

Christmas in Silver Bell Falls
Christmas On Pointe

## Life, Love & Babies Series:

The Baby Arrangement
Baby, Be Mine
Baby, I'm Yours

## Preston's Mill Series:

Roommating
Speed Dating

## The Protectors Series:

Duty Bound
Honor Bound
Forever Bound
Home Bound

## Standalone Novels:

Jordan's Return
Catering to the CEO
In the Eye of the Storm
A Touch of Heaven
Moonlight in Winter Park

Wildest Dreams
Going My Way
Going to Be Yours
Waiting for Midnight
Seeking Forever
Mistletoe Between Friends
Snowflake Inn Wedding

*Enjoy the following excerpt for*

# Christmas in Silver Bell Falls

A Silver Bell Falls Holiday Novella

## Chapter One

There was nothing quite like coming home at the end of a long day: kicking off your shoes…having a little something to eat while watching TV…and most importantly, not having to hear any more Christmas music!

Melanie Harper was certain she wasn't the only one who felt that way. It was early November and the holiday season was just getting under way.

"More like under my skin," she murmured as she walked into her kitchen and poured herself a glass of wine. Taking her glass, she went back to her living room and sat down on the couch.

It had been a long day. A long week. Hell, if she were being honest, it had been a long three months. With deadlines approaching, her editor was getting more and more snarky while Melanie was getting more and more discouraged.

Writer's block.

In her ten years of writing, she'd never once suffered from it, but for some reason the words refused to come.

"Figures," she said with disgust and turned on the TV. Flipping through the channels, it was all the same thing—Christmas specials, Christmas movies and holiday-themed shows. Unable to stand it, she turned it off and sighed.

It was always like this. Christmas. The holidays. Every year, if something bad was going to happen, it happened around Christmas.

Not that it had been that way her entire life, but…she stopped and paused. No, scratch that. It had been like that her entire life. Her earliest memory was of the Christmas when she was five. That was the year her mother left. Her father had been too distraught to celebrate that year so she spent the day watching him drink and cry.

There had been a glimmer of hope for the next year—her dad promised her it would be better. The flu had both of them fighting for the bathroom the entire day. And after that, it was all one big, giant blur of suckiness. Between financial struggles and family issues—and that one year where they had gotten robbed the day before Christmas—Melanie had come to see the months of November and December as nothing but a big nuisance. Eventually they stopped even attempting to celebrate.

And now she'd be able to add "getting cut by her publisher because of writer's block" to the Christmas resume of doom.

The name almost made her chuckle.

It would have been easy to sit there and wax unpoetic about how much she hated this time of the year, but a knock at the door saved her. Placing her wine glass down, she padded to the front door and pulled it open.

"Hey! There's my girl!"

Melanie smiled as her dad wrapped her in his embrace. "Hey, Dad." She hugged him back and then stepped aside so he could come in. "What's going on? I thought we were getting together on

Saturday for dinner."

John Harper smiled at his only child as he took off his coat. "Is this a bad time?"

She shook her head. "No, not at all. I just wasn't expecting you. Have you eaten dinner yet?"

He chuckled softly. "It's almost eight, Mel. Of course I have." He studied her for a minute. "Don't tell me you haven't."

She shrugged. "It was a long day and I sort of lost my appetite."

"Uh-oh. What happened?"

Melanie led him to the living room and sat down on the couch again. "My deadline will be here at the end of December and I haven't written a thing."

"Okay," he said slowly. "So...can't they extend your deadline?"

She shook her head. "They've extended it three times already."

"Hmm...so what's the problem with the story? Why are you having such a hard time with it? That's not like you."

She sighed again. "They're pretty much demanding a Christmas story."

"Oh."

She didn't even need to look at him to know his expression was just as pinched as hers at the topic. "Yeah...oh."

"Did you try explaining...?"

Nodding, she sat up and reached for her glass of wine. "Every time I talk to them. They don't get it and they don't care. Basically their attitude is that I'm a fiction writer and I should be able to use my imagination to concoct this Christmas story without having to draw on personal experience."

"Maybe they don't realize just how much you dislike the holiday."

"Dislike is too mild of a word," she said flatly. Taking a long drink, she put her glass down and looked at him. "I don't even want to talk about it. The meeting with my editor and agent went on and on and on today so my brain is pretty fried. The only thing to come out of it is yet another crappy reinforcement of the holiday."

"Oh, dear…"

Melanie's eyes narrowed. "What? What's wrong?"

"I guess maybe I should have called first because…" He stopped. "You know what? Never mind. We'll talk on Saturday." He stood quickly and walked back toward the foyer.

"Oh, no," she said as she went after him. "You can't come here and say something like that and then leave! Come on. What's going on?"

John sighed and reached for her hand. "Your grandmother died."

Melanie simply stared at him for a minute. "Oh…okay. Wow. Um…when?"

"A month ago."

Her eyes went wide. "And you're just telling me now?"

Slowly, he led her back to the couch. "Mel, seriously? Your grandmother hasn't spoken to me in over twenty-five years. I'm surprised I was notified."

"I guess," she sighed. Then she looked at him.

"Are you okay?"

He shrugged. "I'm not sure. I always thought when the time came that it wouldn't mean anything. After all, she kind of died to me all those years ago. But now? Now that I know she's really gone?" His voice choked with emotion. "It all suddenly seems so stupid, so wrong. I mean, how could I have let all those years go by without trying to make things right?"

Squeezing his hand, Melanie reached over and hugged him. "It's not like you never tried, Dad. Grandma was pretty stubborn. You can't sit here and take all the blame."

When she released him, she saw him wipe away a stray tear. "In my mind, I guess I always thought there would be time. Time to make amends and..."

"I know," she said softly. "And I'm sorry. I really am."

"You probably don't even remember her. You were so little when it all happened."

It was the truth, sort of. Melanie had some memories of her grandmother and none of them were of the warm and fuzzy variety. Unfortunately, now wasn't the time to mention it. "So who contacted you?"

"Her attorney. He actually called last night and met me in person today."

"Well that was nice of him. I guess."

"He had some papers for me. For us."

Melanie looked at him oddly. "What kind of papers?"

"She um...she left some things to us in her

will."

Her eyes went wide again. "Seriously? The woman didn't talk to either of us all these years and she actually put us in her will? Is it bad stuff?"

John chuckled. "What do you mean by bad stuff?"

"You know…like she has a really old house and she was a hoarder and we're supposed to clean it out. Or she has some sort of vicious pet we're supposed to take care of. That kind of thing."

John laughed even harder. "Sometimes your imagination really is wild; you know that, right?" he teased.

Melanie couldn't help but laugh with him. "What? It's true! Things like that happen all the time!"

"Mel, it doesn't," he said, wiping the tears of mirth from his eyes. "And for your information, there was no hoarding, no vicious pets…"

"Did she collect dead animals or something?"

He laughed again. "No. Nothing like that."

Relaxing back on the couch, she looked at her father. "Okay. Lay it on me then. What could she possibly have put in her will for the two of us?"

John took a steadying breath. "She left me my father's coin collection."

That actually made Melanie smile. "I know how much you used to talk about it." She nodded with approval. "That's a good gift to get."

He nodded. "She'd kept it all these years. Then there's some family photos, things from my childhood that she had saved, that sort of thing."

"So no money," Melanie said because she

already knew the answer.

John shook his head. "And it's fine with me. I don't think I would have felt comfortable with it. All those years ago, it would have meant the world to me to have a little help so you and I didn't have to struggle so much. But we're good now and I don't really need or want it."

"Who'd she leave it to? Her cat? Some snooty museum?"

"Museums aren't snooty," he said lightly.

"Anyway," she prompted. "So who'd she leave her fortune to?"

With a sigh he took one of her hands in his. "She left the bulk of her estate to the local hospice care center."

"Oh...well...that was nice of her," Melanie said. "I guess she wasn't entirely hateful."

"No, she wasn't," John said softly. "And she did leave you something."

The statement wasn't a surprise since he'd mentioned it earlier, but Melanie figured he'd tell her when he was ready.

"When the attorney told me about it," he began, "I was a little surprised. I had no idea she still had it."

Curiosity piqued, she asked, "Had what?"

"The cabin."

Okay, that was a surprise, she thought. "Grandma had a cabin? Where?"

"Up north. Practically on the border of Canada."

"Seriously? Why on earth would she have a cabin there?"

A small smile played across John's face. "Believe it or not, there was a time when your grandmother wasn't quite so...hard. She loved the winters and loved all of the outdoor activities you could do in the snow. She skied, went sleigh riding and...get this...she loved Christmas."

Pulling her hand from his, Melanie stood with a snort of disgust. "That's ironic. The woman went out of her way to ruin so many of our Christmases and now you're telling me she used to love them? So...so...what? She started hating them after I came along? That would just be the icing on the rotten Christmas cookie."

John came to his feet and walked over to her. Placing his hands on her shoulders, he turned her to look at him. "It wasn't you, sweetheart. It was me. When your mom left, grandma wanted us to move in with her—but there were conditions and rules and I just knew it wasn't the kind of environment I wanted you to grow up in."

"Dad, I know all this. I remember the fights but...what made her hate Christmas?"

He shook his head. "She didn't. As far as I know, she always loved it."

"Then...then why? Why would she ruin ours?"

A sad expression covered his face. "It was punishment. I grew up loving Christmas and we always made such a big celebration out of it. It was her way of punishing me for not falling in line. She took away that joy."

Tears filled Melanie's eyes. "See? She was hateful. And whatever this cabin thing is, I don't want it."

"Mel…"

"No, I'm serious!" she interrupted. "I don't want anything from her. She ruined so many things in our lives because she was being spiteful! Why on earth would I accept anything from her?"

"Because I think you need it," he said, his tone firm, serious.

"Excuse me?"

Leading her back to the sofa, they sat down. "I think this may have come at the perfect time."

She rolled her eyes. "Seriously?"

"Okay, that didn't quite come out the way I had planned," he said with a chuckle. "What I meant is…I think you could really use the time away. With the pressure you're feeling about the book, maybe a change of scenery will really help put things into perspective."

"Dad," Melanie began, "a change of scenery is not going to undo twenty-five years of hating Christmas. And besides, I really don't want the…the cabin. I don't want anything from her. It would have meant more to me to have her in my life while she was alive."

He sighed. "I know and I wish things could have been different. But…this is really something you need to do."

She looked at him with disbelief. "Now I need to do it? Why?"

"Melanie, you are my daughter and I love you."

"That's an ominous start."

"You're too young to be this disillusioned and angry. We can't go back and change anything, but I think you need to do this to make peace with the past and have some hope for the future."

"Dad..."

"Three months, Mel, that's all I'm asking."

She jumped to her feet. "You expect me to go live in some arctic place for three months? Are you crazy?"

He smiled patiently at her. "I'm not crazy and you know I'm right."

"No...I'm still going with crazy."

"There's a stipulation in the will," he began cautiously.

"What kind of stipulation?"

"You need to live in the cabin for three months. After that, you're free to sell it."

"That's a bunch of bull. What if I don't want to live there at all? Why can't I just sell it now? Or give it away?"

"If you don't want it, it will be given away."

"Well then...good riddance."

"You're being spiteful just for the sake of it, Mel. What have you got to lose? You work from home so you don't have that hanging over your head and your condo is paid for. Think of it as a writing retreat. Your editor will love the idea and it will show how you're seriously trying to get the book done. It's a win-win if you think about it."

"Ugh," she sighed. "I'm not a big fan of being cold."

"The cabin has heat."

"It will mean I'll be gone for Christmas."

He chuckled. "Nice try. We don't celebrate it anymore, remember?"

She let out a small growl of frustration. "I'm

still going to have writer's block. That's not going to change."

"Trust me. It will."

Tilting her head, she gave him a curious look. "What's that supposed to mean?"

"Okay, there really isn't any way not to tell you this…"

"Tell me what?"

"The town is pretty much all about Christmas."

"Forget it. I'm not going." She sat back down and crossed her arms.

"You're too old to pout so knock it off," he said.

She glared at her father. "So I'm supposed to go to this…this…Christmas town and then, thanks to the wonder of it all, suddenly I'm going to be able to write this fabulous holiday story and have it become a bestseller?"

"There's that imagination again! I knew it was still in there!"

"Ha-ha. Very funny." Slouching down she let out another growl. "I really don't want to do this."

"Mel, it's not often that I put my foot down. You're normally more level-headed and you're old enough that I don't need to, but this time, I'm going to have to put my foot down."

"Who gets the cabin if I turn it down?"

John sighed dejectedly. "I have no idea. The lawyer didn't say."

"Maybe she left it to someone who really needs it," Melanie said, trying to sound hopeful.

"She did," John replied. "You."

A week later, Melanie was in her car and driving halfway across the country to see if she could get her writing mojo back. It was a fifteen-hour drive so she split it up over two days and since she was alone in the car, she had nothing to do but think.

"She couldn't have left me a condo in Hawaii or maybe someplace tropical like the Bahamas? No. I have to go to the tip of freaking New York for this." It was a running dialogue in her head throughout the drive and it seemed like the closer she got, the angrier she became.

On the second day of the trip, when her GPS told her she was less than an hour away from her destination, she called her father and put him on speakerphone.

"Hey, sweetheart! How's the drive?"

"She hated me," Melanie replied. "She seriously hated me."

"I'm not even going to pretend I don't know who you're referring to," he said. "Are you there already? Is the cabin in bad shape?"

"I'm not there yet but I'm driving on this little two-lane road and there is nothing out here. I mean nothing! The GPS says I should be there soon but I haven't seen a city or a town in quite a while. Where am I supposed to shop and get food? Or am I supposed to hunt for it? Because if I am, that's a deal-breaker and you should have told me."

John laughed. "You seriously need to put all of

this in your book. It's hysterical!"

"I'm not trying to be funny here, Dad! I'm serious! There isn't anything around!"

"You haven't gotten there yet. If I remember correctly, there are plenty of places to shop and eat. You won't starve and you certainly won't have to go out and kill your dinner so don't worry."

"But you don't know that for sure…"

"Mel, stop looking for trouble. We talked about this. It's going to be good for you. Your editor is thrilled and promised to give you a little extra time so you're off to a promising start."

"Yeah…I'm lucky," Melanie deadpanned.

"You need a positive attitude, young lady," he admonished. "I'm serious. I want you to make the most of this time you have up there."

She mentally sighed. "I'll try, Dad. But I'm not making any promises."

"That's all I ask."

"Okay, well…let me go because the road seems to be getting pretty winding and hilly and I need to pay attention to it. I'll call you when I get there."

"Be safe, sweetheart!"

Hanging up, Melanie frowned at the road. It was getting narrower and the sky was getting a little bit darker. A chill went down her spine and attributing it to the cooling temperatures, she cranked up the heat.

The GPS began calling out directions to her and Melanie feared she was leaving civilization further and further behind. "I better hit the New York Times for this," she murmured. A few minutes later she hit the brakes and stared at the giant sign on the side of the road.

"Silver Bell Falls Welcomes You!"

Melanie frowned and then looked around because she was certain she was hearing things. Turning down her car stereo, she groaned when she heard the song "Silver Bells" coming from the massive sign.

City sidewalks, busy sidewalks, dressed in holiday style...in the air there's a feeling of Christmas...

"You have got to be kidding me." Cranking the radio up to block out the Christmas carol, Melanie slammed her foot on the gas and continued her drive. It was maybe only a mile down the road when she spotted a small grocery store, a gas station and a diner.

And that was it.

"I guess I just drove through town," she sighed. It was tempting to stop and look around but she was anxious to get to the house and check it out first. Being practical, Melanie had already shopped for enough food and essentials to get her by for the first night. And besides, she had no idea what kind of shape the house was going to be in.

"Turn left," the GPS directed and Melanie did just that. "Your destination is at the end of the road."

Squinting, Melanie looked straight ahead but saw...nothing. There were trees, lots and lots of trees. Slowing down, she approached the end of the pavement and saw a dirt road that led through the trees and a small mailbox hidden in the brush.

"Charming." With no other choice, she

carefully drove off the pavement and made her way over the bumpy road through the trees. It was like a dense forest and for a minute, she didn't think she was going to get through it.

But then she did.

The field opened up and off to the right was a house—not a cabin. In her mind, Melanie pictured some sort of log cabin, but the structure she was looking at was more stone than log. It was a one-story home with a wraparound porch and a red roof. The yard was completely manicured and the place even looked like it had a fresh coat of paint.

Since neither she nor her father had any contact with her grandmother, there was no way for them to know about the upkeep on the place. She had tried to question the lawyer, but other than giving her the deed to the house and the keys, he had very little information for her.

A little beyond the house was a shed. It looked like it was perched on a trailer and it certainly looked a lot newer than the house. Maybe it had been a new addition. Maybe her grandmother hadn't known she was going to die and was doing some renovations on the property.

Pulling up to the front of the house, Melanie sighed. She was anxious to go and explore the space and silently prayed she wasn't going to open the door to some sort of nightmare. Climbing from the car, the first thing she did was stretch. Looking around the property from where she stood, the only thing that was obvious to her was that she had no neighbors—she couldn't even see another house!

Pulling the key from her pocket, she closed the

car door and carefully walked up the two steps to the front porch. Stopping at the front door, she bounced on her feet and noticed that the floor was in pretty good shape—no creaking and a lot of the wood looked fairly new.

Not a bad start, she thought and opened the front door.

Stopping dead in her tracks, she could only stare. It was dark and dusty and there was a smell that made her want to gag. Not that she was surprised, but it did cause her to spring into action. With a hand over her mouth, she quickly made her way around the house opening windows. Next, she went out to her car and grabbed the box of cleaning supplies out of the trunk. Melanie knew a certain amount of cleaning would be involved, but she hadn't expected quite so much.

For the next three hours she scrubbed and dusted and vacuumed and mopped. It didn't matter that it was thirty degrees outside, and currently pushing that temperature inside thanks to the open windows; she was sweating. Once she was satisfied with the way things looked, she walked outside, grabbed the box of linens and went about making the bed. Next came the groceries and finally her own personal belongings.

It was dark outside and every inch of Melanie's body hurt. Slowly she made her way back around the house to close the windows and jacked up the heat. Luckily the fireplace was gas, clearly a recent update. She flipped the switch and sighed with relief when it roared to life and the blower immediately began pushing out heat as well.

Guzzling down a bottle of water, she looked around with a sense of satisfaction. The house was small, maybe only a thousand square feet, but it had potential. Grabbing a banana from her cooler, she peeled and ate it while contemplating her next move.

"Shower," she finally said. "A nice hot shower or maybe a bath." The latter sounded far more appealing. Locking the front door, Melanie walked to the newly-cleaned bathroom and started the bath water. It was a fairly decent-sized tub and for that she was grateful. "Bath salts," she murmured and padded to the master bedroom to search through her toiletry bag.

Within minutes, the bathroom was steamy and fragrant and Melanie could feel the tension starting to leave her body. Her cell phone rang and she cursed when she realized she had forgotten to call her father when she'd arrived.

"Hey, Dad!" she said quickly. "Sorry!"

He chuckled. "Are you all right?"

"I am. The house was a mess and once I got inside and looked around, I couldn't help but start cleaning. I guess I lost track of the time."

"Have you eaten dinner yet?" he asked expectantly.

"A banana."

"Mel..." he whined. "You have to start taking better care of yourself."

"I will. I know. Actually, I'm just getting ready to take a nice hot bath to relax. I promise I'll eat as soon as I'm done."

He sighed wearily. "Okay. Be sure that you

do. Call me tomorrow."

"I will, Dad. Thanks."

She hung up and turned the water off. Looking around, Melanie grabbed some fresh towels from one of her boxes and set them on the vanity before stripping down and gingerly climbing into the steamy water. A groan of pure appreciation escaped her lips as soon as she was fully submerged.

"This almost makes up for all the grime," she sighed and rested her head back, closing her eyes. "Heavenly."

For a few minutes, Melanie let her mind be blank and simply relaxed. The hot water and the salts were doing wonders for her tired body and it was glorious. Then, unable to help herself, her mind went back into work mode. A running list of supplies she was going to need was first and she cursed not having a pad and pen handy to start writing things down. Next came the necessities of going into town and maybe meeting her neighbors.

And then there was the book.

The groan that came out this time had nothing to do with relaxation and everything to do with dread. "Damn Christmas story. Why can't I write what I want to write?" It was something she'd been asking her editor for months and the only response she got was how all of the other in-house authors were contributing to building their holiday line, and she would be no exception. "Stupid rule."

And then something came to her.

Melanie sat up straight in the tub and only mildly minded the water that sloshed over the side of the tub. "All I need to do is write a story that takes place around Christmas. It doesn't have to necessarily be about Christmas!" Her heart began to beat frantically. "I've been focusing on the wrong thing!" Relief swamped her and she forced herself to relax again. Sinking back into the water, she closed her eyes and let her mind wander to all of the possibilities that had suddenly opened up.

"A romance at Christmas time," she said quietly. "Major emphasis on romance, minor on Christmas. Technically, I'm meeting my obligations." She smiled. "Hmm...a heroine alone—maybe stranded—in a winter storm and a sexy hero who storms in and rescues her."

Melanie purred. "Yeah. That could definitely work." Sinking further down into the water, an image of the hero came to mind. Tall. That was a given. Muscular, but not overly so. Maybe lean would be a better way to describe him. And dark hair. She was a sucker for the dark hair. "Sex on a stick," she said quietly, enjoying the image that was playing in her mind.

The bathroom door swung open and Melanie's eyes flew open as she screamed. The man standing in the doorway seemed to have stepped almost completely from her imagination. If she wasn't so freaking scared at the moment, she would appreciate it.

"I wouldn't count on sex on a stick or anyplace else if I were you. You're trespassing and you're under arrest."

Made in the USA
Columbia, SC
06 July 2022